EMILY & JACKSON
HIDING OUT

EMILY & JACKSON HIDING OUT

PHYLLIS REYNOLDS NAYLOR

ILLUSTRATED BY ROSS COLLINS

DELACORTE PRESS

Text copyright © 2012 by Phyllis Reynolds Naylor
Jacket art copyright © 2012 by Greg Call
Interior illustrations copyright © 2012 by Ross Collins

Visit us on the Web! randomhouse.com/kids
Educators and librarians, for a variety of teaching tools,
visit us at RHTeachersLibrarians.com

Library of Congress Cataloging-in-Publication Data
Naylor, Phyllis Reynolds.
Emily and Jackson hiding out / Phyllis Reynolds Naylor. — 1st ed.
p. cm.
Summary: Things start looking up for Emily and Jackson when Emily's inheritance clears and Aunt Hilda becomes her legal guardian and offers to become Jackson's, as well, but Uncle Victor reappears, willing to do anything to steal Emily's fortune.
ISBN 978-0-385-74097-5 (hardback) — ISBN 978-0-375-98342-9 (ebook)
ISBN 978-0-375-98978-0 (glb)
[1. Adventure and adventurers—Fiction. 2. Foster parents—Fiction.
3. Kidnapping—Fiction. 4. Inheritance and succession—Fiction. 5. Orphans—Fiction. 6. West (U.S.)—History—19th century—Fiction.] I. Title.
PZ7.N24Elh 2012   [Fic]—dc23   2011044335

The text of this book is set in 14-point Bodoni.

Printed in the United States of America
10 9 8 7 6 5 4 3 2 1
First Edition

For my grandsons,
Beckett and Garrett,
who love books

CONTENTS

ONE
Redbud

Emily was about the happiest thing alive.

When she and her friend Jackson got to her aunt Hilda's, they whooped and they hollered. They ran around half-crazy with gladness.

They chased the dog and scared the chickens, circled the sheep and made the cows moo. They waded in the creek to look for crawdads, and finally, when they were almost too tired to spit, they lay in the grass and studied the sky.

"That Victor was mean as a snake," Jackson said

after a bit. "Where do you suppose he is now—him and his tiger tattoo?"

"Far away from here, I hope," said Emily, remembering how her uncle Victor had followed them all the way to Redbud, trying to get the fortune Emily had inherited when her mother died. "It's hard to believe he's my mother's brother, when she was always so sweet and kind."

"Sure wish I could remember *my* ma," said Jackson. "Guess we're just two motherless kids out in the world alone."

"Not anymore!" said Emily. "Now we have Aunt Hilda."

It was about then that Emily and Jackson decided they were hungry. They could hear their stomachs growling back and forth to each other, having a real conversation. The minute the two children got up, the friendly black dog got up too, his red tongue hanging out, and loped along after them.

Aunt Hilda was standing in the doorway of her little white cottage. Her hands were resting on her plump hips, and her smile was as wide as her face.

"Well, young'uns," she said. "How do you like it here in Redbud?"

"Like it fine," said Jackson. "And I like this here dog too."

"Name's Spook," Aunt Hilda said, "because everywhere you go, he's right behind you. Wash your hands at the pump, now, and set yourselves down at the table."

They did just as she said, and what a feast she had prepared! There were beans and ham, potatoes and peas, biscuits with honey, and fresh apple pie for dessert.

Jackson looked like a chipmunk, his cheeks were so full. Each time he reached for something more, Emily saw him glance at Aunt Hilda to see if she would stop him. But Aunt Hilda only smiled.

After the pie was served, she said, "Now that we're a family, let's go over the rules of this house: Everybody has work to do, even Spook. He herds the sheep and brings the cows in from pasture. Jackson's jobs are to keep the wood box and the water bucket full. Emily's jobs are to sweep the floors and make the beds. I'll do most of the rest. There will be extra chores from time to time, but most important of all, we practice kindness. If you see any suffering creature, two-legged or four-, you do what you can to help."

"Yes, ma'am," said Emily, because she had been taught to be polite.

Jackson only nodded, because his mouth was full of pie.

• • •

After supper, Aunt Hilda washed the dishes and Emily and Jackson dried them. Then the two children worked on the little pen they were making for Rufus, Emily's pet turtle. And finally, when night began to fall and even the crickets sounded tired, Aunt Hilda said it was time for bed—Emily in the small room all fixed up for her next to the kitchen, and Jackson in the loft above the parlor, with the little ladder he would climb to get up there, and the tiny window where he could look out and see the stars.

"But first," Emily's aunt told them, "both of you are going to get a good scrubbing. I don't think I have ever seen two dirtier children."

Jackson was sent into the parlor to wait his turn, and Emily took off her clothes, all dusty and caked with mud. Aunt Hilda pulled a tin tub into the middle of the kitchen floor. She poured cold water from the bucket, then hot water from the teakettle, until the temperature was just right. Emily stepped in and sat down, and soon she was covered with soap bubbles from the top of her head to the tips of her toes.

Her hair was all raggedy. Jackson had cut it during their trip to Redbud, when they'd been trying to disguise Emily as a boy. He had even given her some of his clothes to wear. But Uncle Victor had recognized her anyway, and he'd tried everything he could think of to stop Emily from reaching Aunt Hilda. Fortunately, nothing had worked.

I won't have to worry about Uncle Victor ever again, Emily told herself as Aunt Hilda scrubbed her back with a long-handled brush and Emily worked on her fingernails with a short one.

"You're good as new, Emily!" her aunt said finally, when Emily was in her nightgown, sweet-smelling and dry. "And I reckon you're going to sleep well tonight after all your adventures."

Scrub brush in hand, Aunt Hilda opened the door to the parlor, with Emily right behind her, to tell Jackson he was next.

And what in gigglin' goblins do you think they saw?

TWO

Ten Million Dollars

Jackson was not in a chair.

He was not on the sofa.

He was sitting in the loft, his legs dangling over the edge, and he had pulled the ladder up after him.

"Jackson?" Aunt Hilda said. "Your turn."

Jackson only shook his head.

Emily could not believe this.

"Come on down here, boy," Aunt Hilda told him.

"No," said Jackson, scooting back against the wall. "I didn't do nothing!"

"What are you talking about?" Aunt Hilda asked.

"I'm not gettin' any beating with a brush," Jackson declared.

Emily's aunt looked down at the scrub brush in her hand and then up at Jackson. "Why, child, I'm not about to beat you!" she said. "The only thing this brush will do is scrub you clean. I've never beaten a child before, and I'm not starting now. Please won't you come down?"

Jackson slowly lowered the ladder and climbed down, watching Aunt Hilda over his shoulder. When he reached the floor, she put an arm around him and led him into the kitchen. "And once you two are tucked in," she said, "I'm going to wash your clothes up good and clean so you'll have a fresh start tomorrow in your new home."

• • •

The days went on, bright and sunny. There was always something for the children to do around Aunt Hilda's place.

A white picket fence surrounded the cottage, the barn, and the flower and vegetable gardens. It went all the way to the gate at the end of the lane. Just beyond the picket fence was the post-and-wire fence that bordered the grassland where the sheep and cows grazed. And running around the back of all the property, yard and pasture both, were the creek and woods.

Emily and Jackson explored everything there was to see—the windmill, the well, the barn, the shed; the springhouse, the meadow, the sheepfold, the creek. They rode Old Billy, the horse, and taught Spook to sit up and beg. They added a rock and a cave to Rufus's pen, and watched the turtle climb onto the rock to sun himself. Emily's hair grew longer, her arms and legs stronger, and Jackson gained ten pounds right off.

Jackson was the curious one. He liked to peep through every keyhole, look in every box, check out every cupboard, and open every door—even the heavy door to the storm cellar, which was outside next to the house. If there was a crank to turn, he cranked it. If there was a rope to pull, he yanked it.

Jackson was the hungry one too. He was always first at the table when it was time for supper.

One day Emily received a letter saying that the

ten million dollars she had inherited was now in the
bank. She would have to ride to the bank in town with

Aunt Hilda to sign some papers to make it official—
and to name her aunt her legal guardian.

Emily was thrilled. She didn't like to talk about the
money, because it made her think about her mother.
And thinking about her mother made her sad. But,
at last, she belonged someplace where she was loved
again! That was more important than the money. She
knew her aunt would love her even if she didn't have
a penny.

"I still don't understand it," Emily said as she and
Aunt Hilda started off the next morning. Jackson
stayed behind to paint the gate. "The bank said that
the ten million dollars belonged to my mother, but she
never had much money at all."

"It works like this, Emily," her aunt explained,
pulling at the reins so Old Billy would keep to his side
of the road. "The woman your mother worked for was

very, very rich, and she had no husband or children. She had made out a will saying that when she died, all of her money should go to your mother, for her long and faithful service. But when they both died in the same accident, the ten million dollars became yours, because you are your mother's only child."

"But if it belongs to me, why did Uncle Victor think he could get it?" Emily asked, remembering the man with the silver-black hair of a wolf and the eyes of a weasel and the growl of a bear and a big tiger tattoo on one arm.

"Since he's your mother's brother, he thought he could be named your legal guardian, and then he could decide how to spend it," said Aunt Hilda. "And I'm afraid he wanted to spend it all on himself."

"I would rather have my mother back than a million billion dollars," Emily said in a small voice.

"Of course, dear, but now we have to decide what to do with it," Aunt Hilda said.

"I already know," Emily told her. "I want to give it all to you. Jackson said it's enough to buy a ranch."

Aunt Hilda chuckled. "Gracious, child, it would

buy ten ranches, and more. But Redbud's just the right size for me, and now that I've got you and Jackson, I can't think of a whole lot more I need. We have to make sure that money's nice and safe so it will be waiting for you when you're all grown up and needing it for yourself."

When they reached the bank, Emily was seated at a big table with lawyers to the left of her and lawyers to the right. The bank president sat at the head of the table. Each lawyer in turn picked up a paper and read it to Emily, then handed her a pen and showed her where to sign her name.

"Now, Emily," said the bank president in his high-collared shirt and his glasses that rested on the end of his nose, "your money is safe in this bank, and your aunt Hilda is your trustee. That means she will help you decide how and when to spend it. But would you like some of it now?"

Emily looked at her aunt. "Could we stop at the chocolate shop and get something for Jackson?" she asked.

"Indeed we could," said Aunt Hilda. "And it might

be a good idea to take some of the money home with us so it will be handy if we ever need it in a hurry."

And because Aunt Hilda needed a new harness for Old Billy and a new roof for the barn and even a new pony, by and by, to help out, the men at the bank suggested that she take five hundred dollars home and keep it in a safe place.

After Emily and her aunt left, they stopped at the candy store to buy not only chocolates for Jackson and vanilla crèmes for Emily and Aunt Hilda, but also two brightly colored kites, one yellow and one green.

Back outside again, they had just turned the corner when Emily heard a loud *clatter-clatter-rattle-rattle*.

What in leapin' loonies do you think it was?

THREE

Hole in the Ground

It was a gray carriage drawn by a gray horse. And on the side of the carriage, printed in big bold letters, were the words:

CATCHUM CHILD-CATCHING SERVICES
REDBUD DIVISION
ORPHANS, STRAYS, AND ROUSTABOUTS
ROUNDED UP QUICKLY

Out of habit, Emily ducked behind Aunt Hilda, clutching her aunt's big friendly arm in one hand and the new guardianship papers in the other.

"Why, child, whatever is the matter?" Aunt Hilda said. "They're not after you. I'm your legal guardian now. That's settled and done with."

"How can we be sure?" Emily asked as the gray carriage stopped and a man in a gray suit stepped out, looking first one way, then the other.

With a firm grip on Emily's hand, Aunt Hilda marched right over to the man.

"Would you be needing any help?" she asked. "You seem to be looking for someone."

Emily found herself shaking just from being close to the child catchers.

"Indeed I am," said the man. "My agency is looking for a young rascal named Jackson, nine years old. A stagecoach driver said he'd got off here at Redbud and hasn't been seen since."

"Oh, really?" said Aunt Hilda. "And what has the rascal done?"

"He's being sent to a family out west who needs a

boy to work in their mill," said the man. "He knows he can't stop off along the way."

"I wouldn't think a boy of nine was old enough to work in a mill," said Aunt Hilda.

"Well, that's not my problem," said the gray-suited man. Even his voice sounded gray. "An orphan child should be glad for any roof at all over his head. It looks like he's given us the slip. But we'll find him, don't think we won't. If you see a hungry-looking lad with no place to sleep, I'd be obliged if you'd let us know."

"I'll certainly keep an eye out for him," Aunt Hilda said. The driver got back into the gray carriage and shook the reins, and the gray horse started off again.

Emily looked up at her aunt in horror. "You won't give Jackson to them, will you?" she asked.

Aunt Hilda led Emily over to their horse and wagon and climbed up. "I didn't say I would, did I? I said I'd keep an eye out for Jackson, and believe me, I will. An eye out to see that those Catchum folks don't catch him. And as you can see, they're not after you."

On the way home, Emily said, "That was how I first met Jackson. Before I got on the stagecoach to come to you, I was trying to hide from the child catchers, and I bumped into him. Jackson had a ticket for the stagecoach too, and all the way here, he helped me hide from them, and from Uncle Victor too."

"You're safe with me," said Aunt Hilda, "and Jackson can stay as long as he likes."

"Forever?" asked Emily.

"If he wants to," said her aunt.

• • •

It was a fun afternoon. Jackson and Emily flew their kites so high that they let out all the string. They tied the ends to a fence post, then sat under a tree eating the candy Emily had bought, watching the kites bob about in the sky.

"What's it like to be rich?" Jackson asked after a while.

"Feels pretty much like yesterday," Emily answered. "And same as the day before that."

"Yeah, but now you can have anything you want," Jackson told her.

"No, I can't. I can't have my mother back," Emily said. And they grew quiet.

After supper that evening, Aunt Hilda cleared the table and sat the two children down, one on either side of her.

"We've got us five hundred dollars here to use as we need it, and I'd like your ideas on a good hiding place," she said. "If anything happens to me, you children need to know where to find it."

"Could stick it under your mattress," said Jackson.

"Very first place a thief would look," Aunt Hilda said.

"What about the flour bin?" asked Emily.

"Second place he'd look," replied her aunt.

"A hole in the ground?" Emily and Jackson said together.

"You know, I had the same idea," said Aunt Hilda. "We could bury it out in the yard. I've got an empty coffee tin and a wood box I used once as a birdhouse. We could put the money in the tin, the tin in the box, and the box in the ground, then roll a heavy rock over the top to mark the spot."

So they chose a place halfway between the barn and the cottage. Aunt Hilda got a shovel and they took turns digging a hole, huffing and puffing, as Spook lay in the grass and watched.

All at once there was a *clink*. Aunt Hilda tossed out the dirt and thrust the shovel in again. *Clunk*, they heard this time. Aunt Hilda reached down and pushed the dirt aside.

And what in flirtin' floozies do you suppose she found?

FOUR

Good Luck, Bad Luck

"Well, blow me over!" said Aunt Hilda as the three of them stared down into the hole.

It was a watch. A gold watch on a gold chain. When Aunt Hilda picked it up and rubbed it against her apron, it gleamed as good as new.

"Sam's pocket watch!" the big woman said softly. "My husband, Sam, lost this a week before he died. We looked for it all over the place, but he'd dropped it somewhere, and I guess the somewhere was here."

"But . . . how did it get down in a hole?" asked Jackson.

"That was a long time ago," said Aunt Hilda. "The wind blew dust over it, I guess, and when the rain came, grass grew over it and the watch just sank deeper and deeper."

She held the pocket watch against her cheek and

kissed it. "Oh, how I've wanted to find this. It was the dearest thing he had, next to me."

"H-how did he die?" asked Emily hesitantly.

"A big old tree fell on him," said Aunt Hilda, wiping her eyes. "A hurricane blew in off the Gulf—wind and rain like you wouldn't believe. Our little house took it okay, but all that water loosened the roots of some of the trees. And the next day, when Sam was down by the river, a cottonwood just blew over and hit him. Oh, but that was a sad day for me."

Emily put her arms around her aunt and hugged her tight, but Jackson stood there uneasily, staring at the watch.

"Would you like to hold it?" Aunt Hilda asked him.

Jackson shook his head and backed away.

"What's the matter, child?" Aunt Hilda said.

"It's bad luck," said Jackson.

"Bad luck to find a watch that's been missing for twenty years?" said Aunt Hilda. "Seems like good luck to me."

"The hands are at midnight," said Jackson. "That's bad luck for sure."

Aunt Hilda stared at Jackson, then at the watch. "Now, how do you know that watch might not be showing noontime, not midnight? Didn't know you were superstitious, Jackson."

"I know bad luck when I see it, 'cause I've sure had plenty," Jackson told her.

"Well," said Aunt Hilda, giving the watch a final pat and dropping it in her apron pocket, "I'd say that today is a lucky day. And we've got us five hundred dollars here, so let's finish the job."

They set to work digging again, and when the hole was wide enough, Aunt Hilda took the coffee tin with the money in it and placed it in the wooden box that used to be a birdhouse. She closed the lid and set the box in the hole.

The three of them filled the hole with dirt, patted it down, then scattered leaves and twigs over the dirt. Finally they rolled a big rock on top of it.

"There!" said Aunt Hilda, clapping her hands together to shake off the dirt. "That's our little nest egg. Now I've got us some sausages for our supper, so let's eat!"

• • •

That evening, after the two children were in their nightclothes, Aunt Hilda took her husband's gold watch from her pocket and gently placed it in the little drawer of the lamp table.

"Now I've got something of Sam's right here in this room with me," she said. "Maybe I'll even wind it once in a while and listen to it tick."

And because it had been such an eventful day, she let Emily climb up the ladder to the loft where Jackson slept, so that she could look out for a bit and see the stars.

It was a particularly bright night. Emily and Jackson lay on their stomachs, looking up.

"Ever think about who else is maybe looking at

the same stars in the same sky?" Jackson asked.

That seemed like a strange question to Emily. "Hundreds and hundreds of people," she said.

"Could be people you never want to see again, like your uncle Victor, looking at the same stars in the same sky at the very same time you are, and you don't even know it."

"I hope not," said Emily. "It could also be somebody you miss very much." She rolled over on her back and looked at the stars upside down. They were just as bright as they were right-side up. "Who do *you* miss the most?" she asked.

Jackson thought for a while. "Guess I miss havin' someone to miss. Didn't ever get to know my pa, and my ma ran off when I was little."

"Then who took care of you?" asked Emily.

"I was just tossed from one family to the next— nobody wanted another mouth to feed. They said I caused more trouble than I was worth," Jackson told her. "Can't have been *too* much trouble, 'cause I wasn't worth very much."

"That's not true," said Emily. "If it weren't for you, Uncle Victor would have taken me with him and tried to become my guardian. You're worth a lot to *me*."

"Well, finally they just turned me over to the child catchers and told them to find me a place to live," Jackson continued. "Those Catchum folks get a bonus when they find a boy to work hard at something nobody else wants to do."

"That's awful!" said Emily. "Why don't you ask Aunt Hilda to be your guardian?"

"And what would that mean?" asked Jackson. "That she would own me like a dog?"

Emily rolled over again and sat up. She studied Jackson's face in the moonlight. "It wouldn't mean she owned you, Jackson. It would mean you belonged. Just like I belong now."

Jackson let out his breath. "I don't know," he said. "Never really belonged to anyone before, and don't know if I'd like it."

Suddenly Emily cried, "Jackson! Look!" She pointed out the window.

And what in jumpin' Joseph do you think they saw?

FIVE

Jackson's Mistake

Jackson looked just in time to see it too—a shooting star. A streak of light moved over the dark sky and, just as suddenly, it was gone.

"I made a wish!" Emily said.

"Why?" asked Jackson.

"When you see a shooting star and you make a wish before it's gone, the wish will come true," Emily told him.

"Who's superstitious *now*?" said Jackson.

"Well, I think something good *is* going to happen," said Emily.

"It already has. You got ten million dollars," Jackson said. "What did you wish?"

But Emily wouldn't tell. "It's a secret," she said. She had wished that Aunt Hilda would become Jackson's legal guardian. That, however, was up to her aunt and Jackson.

• • •

Every morning, Emily got up and made the beds before breakfast. She happily swept the floor and dusted the furniture, and always asked if there was anything more she could do to help before she went out to play.

Jackson too was doing his part. At first, Emily had thought he might try to get out of the jobs Aunt Hilda had given him. If there was any way Jackson could get into trouble, he usually did. So far, though, he had brought in wood for the stove each morning, and he filled the water bucket when it was getting low. He did it all without complaining.

Sometimes Aunt Hilda asked him to pick some beans from her garden, or ride Old Billy around the pasture to check the fence. And each new chore Jackson learned to do seemed to make him stronger.

It was amazing to Emily how many things Aunt Hilda and her husband had made themselves when Sam was alive.

"Why buy it if you can make it yourself?" Aunt Hilda liked to say.

She had made their mattress by sewing two sheets together to make a huge bag and filling it with cotton. Sam had made a beehive from a large wooden box, and bees buzzed happily in and out, making honey. Aunt Hilda and Uncle Sam had made a scarecrow out of Sam's old clothes and tied it to a pole in the garden. They had put up their own fence, built their own shed, sewn their own curtains, and gone fishing with only a long stick and some string. And because Hilda liked to swing on warm summer nights, Sam had made a swing for her out of a piece of board and two strong ropes fastened to a high branch on the beech tree.

"I expect there's nothing in this world your aunt can't do herself," said Jackson one afternoon. He was standing on the seat of the swing, one foot on either side of Emily, who was sitting and pumping her legs. Higher and higher they went, the limb of the beech tree rising and falling with the swing. Emily liked to feel the breeze on her face as she swung. Each time the swing went high, she could see far out over the flat countryside to the river. Each time the swing swung low, she pulled her legs up tight so her feet wouldn't scrape the ground.

"I don't think Aunt Hilda could make herself a carriage," Emily said. "She told me that Sam made their big farm wagon, but I'd love for her to have a carriage so she could ride somewhere in the rain if she wanted."

Far out on the road, they saw Aunt Hilda coming back from town, little clouds of dust whirling up behind the wheels of the big wagon.

Emily and Jackson leaped from the swing and went racing down the lane to the gate. Aunt Hilda always had something for them when she came back from a trip to town. Today it was a bag of marbles for Jackson, a finger puppet for Emily, and a little toy palm tree for Rufus, to go in his pen. Even Rufus, tucked in Emily's apron pocket for the swing ride, seemed to know it was market day. When Emily lifted him out, he stretched his little neck as high as it would go, waiting for a raisin from Aunt Hilda.

"I surely have a lot to be thankful for," Emily's aunt said. She carried a big sack of flour into the cottage, and Jackson followed with a sack of cornmeal. As she was putting things away in the cupboard, she said, "A poor old widow woman in her black dress and veil was sitting on the church steps, tin cup in hand. She was still mourning the death of her husband, and needing every penny folks gave her. I'm lucky to have a roof over my head, food in the cupboard, and two young'uns to help out. I surely am."

Later, when they sat down to supper, Aunt Hilda said, "Might be a good idea if you didn't get too close to the road, Jackson. I saw the child catchers in town again today, hunting down stray boys like dogs. If someone was to say you were seen out here at my place, they might just get it in their heads to come after you."

"Isn't no way they could take me from here, is there, now that I got a place to stay?" Jackson asked, reaching for another pork chop.

"Well, I can't exactly keep you here if we're not related, not if they have the papers to send you someplace else," Aunt Hilda said. "Emily, now, she's my niece, so it wasn't hard to make that legal. But you just appeared like a little waterspout over the sea. I'd keep you if I could, but I'd have to have the papers."

"What do we do to get them?" Jackson asked.

"Got to go before the judge and tell him how you came to be an orphan, and whether or not you'd like to live with me," Aunt Hilda said. And when Jackson made no reply, she said, "It's all right. You don't have to decide this minute. Just something to think on."

• • •

The following morning, Aunt Hilda was making a cake and found that she had no eggs.

"I'll be danged if those chickens aren't hiding their eggs from me!" she said when she saw that the egg crate was empty. "I've not an egg to my name. Jackson, would you go out to the barn and see if there are any eggs up in the haymow, where those hens hide 'em sometimes?"

Jackson immediately set out for the barn, and when

Aunt Hilda called after him to take a basket, he just swaggered on, sure he could handle it by himself.

Aunt Hilda waited with her spoon and her bowl, and Emily stood by the door, ready to open it for Jackson when she saw him coming.

A few minutes later, Jackson came out of the barn, walking very slowly, a few pieces of hay in his hair. He had two eggs in one hand, two eggs in the other, and a fifth egg tucked under his chin.

And what in the rooster's rompers do you figure happened next?

SIX

A Terrible Day

What happened next was that the egg under Jackson's chin began to crack, and as he reached up to grab it, he dropped the eggs in his right hand. When he lurched forward to catch those eggs, he dropped the ones in his left hand and went sprawling to the ground on his stomach.

Jackson sat up, wiping the egg off his chin, and Emily could see that all five eggs had broken—five little circles of white and yellow that made sticky puddles there on the dusty ground.

"Are you hurt?" Aunt Hilda asked, coming out the door.

"No, ma'am," said Jackson, "but I guess I should have used a basket."

"Guess you should have," Aunt Hilda said, unsmiling. "And I guess we'll have to forget about the cake."

That was a big disappointment to Emily, and to Jackson too. All week long, Aunt Hilda had said that when she got enough honey from the beehive, she'd make a cake. Now there was honey but no eggs, and Aunt Hilda, who usually hummed while she worked, put the bowl and spoon back in the cupboard. She was not humming now.

Some days, Emily had discovered, started out good and ended up even better. But this day started out bad and got worse.

That evening, when Spook went out to bring the two cows in from the pasture, only one cow came back. Aunt Hilda went to the fence and called in her loudest voice: "Clarabelle? Claaa-raaa-belle? Claaaaaaa-ra!"

But there was no answering moo, and Aunt Hilda went back into the house for her boots and a lantern.

With Emily and Jackson following along behind her, Aunt Hilda walked across the big pasture, the evening sky getting darker and darker. It was hard to see all the bumps and dips in the ground, and Emily's ankles twisted this way and that.

"Clarabelle!" Aunt Hilda kept calling as the lantern swung to and fro. "Come on, bossy!"

When they reached the very end of the pasture, they found that a post had fallen over and the wire fencing had been trampled. It was clear that Clarabelle, the older and smarter cow, had wandered out.

Aunt Hilda turned and faced the two children. "Jackson," she said, "didn't I tell you to get on Old Billy this morning and ride around the whole pasture to make sure none of the fence was down?"

"Yes, ma'am, you did," Jackson answered, his eyes on his feet.

"Then how come this fence post is here on the ground? Looks to me, with weeds growing up over it, that it's been down a right good while."

Emily knew the answer to that. She knew that once Jackson was out of sight of the kitchen window, he was more interested in riding than he was in checking fences.

"I'm sorry," Jackson said.

"Well, we're going to find that cow if it takes us all night," said Aunt Hilda, and they climbed over the broken-down fence, Spook leading the way.

They followed the trampled grass, but the path was getting even more difficult to see.

"If Clarabelle wandered off close to sundown, she can't be too far," Aunt Hilda said. "But if she got out this morning, she could be mighty far from home."

Because the sky was cloudy, there was no moonlight to guide them, only the light from the lantern. Now and then the bushes rustled and a small creature skittered out of the way. An owl hooted and made them jump.

But then, far off, they heard Clarabelle bawling. She needed to be milked, and she probably wanted her supper as much as Emily and Jackson wanted theirs.

Clarabelle was standing down by the creek, her hooves deep in the mud. Aunt Hilda waded in, and with her pushing the cow from behind and Jackson and Emily tugging at Clarabelle's collar, they finally managed to get the stubborn animal back up the bank.

All the way home, Emily wondered if it had been such a good idea to invite Jackson to live with them. She had known since she'd first met him on her long journey to Redbud that he was a boy who got into mischief. Maybe he had caused so much trouble in the other places he had lived that nobody wanted him.

After Clarabelle was safely in the barn again, Aunt Hilda fixed a supper of cold beans and corn bread. She was too tired to cook, and Emily was almost too tired to chew.

No one said
much at the table, and
when Emily laid her head on
her arm and fell asleep, Aunt
Hilda said, "Go to bed, child.
Tomorrow's another day."

Jackson too left the kitchen. While Emily
prepared for bed in her own little
room, she heard the squeak of
the ladder as he climbed up to
the loft.

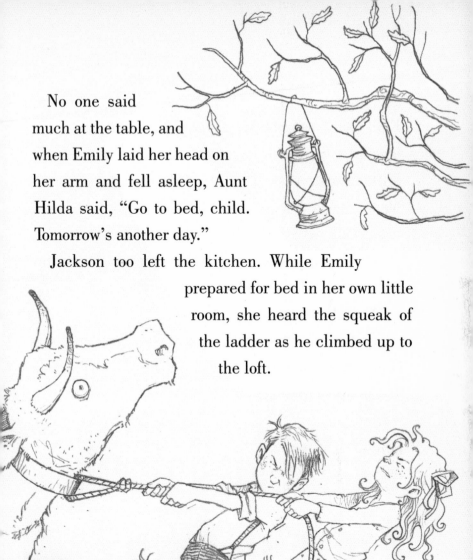

Emily slept soundly all night, waking only when she heard Aunt Hilda calling her and Jackson to breakfast.

She dressed quickly, laced up her high-topped boots, and hurried out to the kitchen. But Jackson, who usually got there first, still wasn't at the table.

Aunt Hilda walked into the parlor and called up into the loft. "Jackson! Get yourself down here, boy."

There was no answer.

"Emily," said her aunt, "would you crawl up there and wake him? A bad day can make you extra tired, and yesterday was a very bad day."

Emily crawled up the ladder, rung by rung.

What in kissin' catfish did she find?

SEVEN

Horseback

Except for the pillow at one end and a blanket at the other, the loft was empty.

Emily looked down at her aunt.

"He's gone!" she said. "And all his things with him."

"Gone?" said Aunt Hilda. "Where could he go?"

Emily climbed back down, looking around the parlor to see if Jackson was playing a trick on them. Hiding behind the sofa, perhaps. But there was no Jackson.

"Well, he can't get far on what little he owned," Aunt Hilda said. "What is he going to do out in the wide world all by himself?"

Emily, however, knew that Jackson was quite used to being in the wide world by himself, sent from one place to another.

"What will he do for food? What will he do for money?" Aunt Hilda said, and suddenly she and Emily turned at the same time and stared at the little drawer in the lamp table.

The gold watch! Emily thought. Jackson could have taken Uncle Sam's watch to sell when he got to town.

Aunt Hilda sighed. "Might as well find out . . . ," she said. She walked over to the table and pulled open the drawer. There was the gold watch, just where she'd left it.

But neither she nor Emily had to say what they were thinking next. They went outside and got a shovel, then rolled away the big rock and dug down to check for the wooden box with the coffee tin inside. And when they opened the tin, there was the five hundred dollars, just where they'd left it.

"I'm ashamed to even have thought he'd steal it," Aunt Hilda said, and she began to weep. "He must be hungry. He must be thirsty too, out on a hot morning like this."

She put the money back and shoveled in the dirt, and then she and Emily rolled the rock into place once again.

"Well," said Aunt Hilda, "I can see now how bad he felt about letting me down—first those eggs and then the cow—but I aim to find him before the child catchers do. Eat your breakfast, Emily, while I saddle up. We're going on horseback in case we have to leave the road and travel the creeks and hills."

• • •

With her legs dangling down on either side and her face against Aunt Hilda's warm back, Emily wrapped her arms around the big woman's waist and off they went on Old Billy—*clip-clop, clip-clop*—down the lane, out the gate, and up the road toward town.

Town was a long way off, however, and Emily had a lot of time to think.

"If Jackson got in trouble everywhere he went,

why are the child catchers so eager to find him?" she asked.

"Because some people are just looking for a body to work, not a child to love," Aunt Hilda said. "And a boy without parents is just the kind of boy they're looking for."

"We could *get* to love him if he stayed around long enough, maybe," said Emily.

"We already do," said Aunt Hilda.

It was indeed a hot day, and even though Emily had put on a big straw hat, she could feel the sun beating down on her back. It was uncomfortable sitting there on the horse behind her aunt, who blocked what little breeze there was.

But Aunt Hilda was hot too, and so was Old Billy as he went clippity-clopping along. Aunt Hilda kept an eye out for Jackson in one direction, and Emily looked in the other. But even though the land was flat as a flapjack, they couldn't see anything that might be a boy—a hungry, thirsty boy with no place to rest. The only way Emily could see straight ahead of her was to lean far out to the left or right. Mostly all she could see was sky—blue sky overhead, but turning darker above the horizon.

They were coming to the crossroad, the only one there was on the way to town. It was the old river road, and it was as empty as the one they were on. If you turned to the right, it led to a swamp. But way to the left, far, far down, Emily thought she saw a little figure moving along that could have been a young boy with a small bundle on his back.

"Aunt Hilda!" she cried. "I think maybe I see him!"

"Where? Where?" Aunt Hilda said, stopping the horse. And then she saw him too—a young boy, plodding along, head down, a little bag thrown over his shoulder.

"I wonder if he has any food or water at all in that bundle," Aunt Hilda said, nudging Old Billy with her legs to start moving again. She pulled the reins to the left.

But just as Emily peered out from behind her aunt to watch their horse make the turn, she saw a little cloud of dust coming down the road straight ahead of them.

Now, what in a bat's belly do you think it was?

EIGHT

Finding Jackson

It was a gray horse pulling a gray carriage, and as it came closer to the crossroad, Emily knew—even before she read the sign on the carriage door—that it was the Catchum Child-Catching Services, Redbud Division.

The gray man in the carriage waved his gray hat as he approached, motioning to them to stop, so they did.

"Good day!" the man said.

"And a good day to you," Aunt Hilda replied.

Hidden behind her aunt, Emily stared to the left

down the crossroad and saw that the little figure that might have been Jackson had disappeared. But if the child catcher turned his carriage that way, he would certainly catch up to whoever was walking down the road.

"Saw you folks in town the other day, didn't I? Heard there was a boy walking along this road early this morning. Wonder if you've seen him," the man said. He waved a bunch of papers in his hand. "Time's

a-wastin', and my agency needs to send him out west, but the boy keeps giving us the slip. A good thrashing he'll get from me when I catch him, you can bet."

Before Aunt Hilda could say a word, Emily jerked around from behind her and said, "There was someone heading far down that way." And she pointed to the right on the old river road. "Don't know if he was big or little."

The man looked puzzled. "*That* way? The road that goes through gullies and gulches and on to the quicksand at Muddy Flats?"

"That's the way he was going," Emily said.

The man tipped his gray hat and turned his horse toward Muddy Flats, the gray carriage bouncing this way and that.

"Well now, Emily, that was a right good yarn, but a lie is still a lie," Aunt Hilda said.

"No, it wasn't!" Emily told her. "I only said there was someone headed that way. I didn't say who and I didn't say when."

Aunt Hilda chuckled as she turned Old Billy to the left, and after a while they saw a little figure get up out of the tall grass and continue walking down the road.

Clip-clop, clip-clop went the horse, and finally they were able to see Jackson clearly, right down to the dusty shoes on his feet.

He didn't turn around when he heard them coming, just plodded on, his bundle over his shoulder, head down.

They pulled up alongside him and Aunt Hilda

slowed Old Billy. "Jackson," she said, "what are you doing way out here, child? Where are you going?"

He gave no answer, but Emily could tell by the way he was dragging his feet that he was tired.

"Wherever you're going, could we take you there?" Aunt Hilda asked kindly, looking down at the dusty boy, whose cap was pulled low over his eyes to keep out the sun. "Looks to me like we've got a storm coming by and by."

"I'm doin' okay by myself," Jackson replied.

For a minute no one spoke as the horse kept pace with Jackson and the shuffle of his tired feet.

"Well," said Aunt Hilda, "if you won't tell us where you're going, will you at least tell us why you left? You owe me that much, Jackson."

Emily saw him take a deep breath. "Always get in trouble no matter where I go. Knew you'd be tellin' me to pack up, so I just figured I'd head out and save you the bother."

Emily started to say something, but Aunt Hilda spoke first: "You know, in this part of the country, it's bad manners to up and leave without saying goodbye.

Now, I see a scrawny little tree up ahead with a bit of shade. I brought along a couple biscuits and a jug of water, and Emily and I are hot and dusty. Will you do us the favor of sitting down in that shade for a drink of water, just for old times' sake?"

Jackson gave a little shrug, but when they reached the shade of the tree, Aunt Hilda guided Old Billy right in front of him so that he had to stop. After she and Emily had gotten off the horse and sat down in the grass, Jackson sat down too, six feet away, his back to them, facing the road. But he took the tin cup of water Aunt Hilda poured for him, and when Emily handed him a biscuit, he took that too.

"Here's the thing, Jackson," Aunt Hilda said. "There's a lot of work to be done on my farm. I don't have a lot of sheep, and when it's lambing or shearing time, some of the neighbor men come over to help. But there's still a lot to do on my own, and if I'd left my farm the first time I did something foolish, I'd have walked off a long time ago."

Jackson stopped chewing. "You would?"

"Sure enough. Why, the day we moved in, Sam and

I had just got our furniture inside, and I went to build a fire in the fireplace, but I didn't think to open the flue. Lit the kindling and the whole house filled with smoke. It was cold January, and we still had to open all the windows to get the smoke out."

"Wow," said Jackson. "That was bad."

"I've done something foolish too," Emily said.

"Not as stupid as carrying an egg under your chin," said Jackson.

But Emily continued: "Yesterday I wore my good shoes to the creek and tried to jump across. I didn't make it." She could feel her cheeks burning even as she told the story. "My very best shoes are under my bed, all muddy."

"Oh, Emily!" said her aunt. "Those were almost new."

"I know," Emily said in a small voice.

"Well," said Aunt Hilda, "shoes are only something to put on your feet, and eggs are only something to put in your stomach. And even if Clarabelle wandered off never to be seen again, Jackson, I'd still rather have a certain boy about the place than any cow."

Jackson turned around and stared at her. "Me?"

"Don't know who else I'd be talking about," she said.

And what in honkin' horntoads do you think Jackson did then?

NINE
Underground

Why, when Aunt Hilda said she'd rather have Jackson than Clarabelle, he gave her a big old hug. The boy who had hardly hugged anyone in his whole life wrapped his arms around the big woman— as far as they would go—and Aunt Hilda hugged right back.

And when she got on the horse and said, "Let's go home," Jackson climbed on right behind her. Emily had to ride at the very back, holding tight to Jackson so she wouldn't slide down the horse's tail. But she was glad to be going home, because the wind was stronger now; it whipped at her skirts and her hair.

Even though she was tired, Aunt Hilda made a lunch of soup and tomato sandwiches, and they listened to the rain hitting the roof as they ate. When the sound became a *rat-a-tat-tat*, Jackson jumped up and ran to the window.

"Wow!" he exclaimed. "There's hail all over the ground!"

Ping, ping, pong, ping went the hail, and Emily joined Jackson, their noses pressed against the glass.

"Whoa!" Jackson cried, jumping backward as a flash of lightning lit up the sky.

"We get these storms now and then, Jackson," Aunt Hilda said. "But if you can still take this wide-open country, just give the word. I'll ride over to the judge one day soon and see what I've got to do to let you live here and be your guardian."

"I'll give the word right now, whatever it is," said Jackson. "I'm right ready to belong somewhere."

"Then I'll find me some time to go get the proper papers, and then you and Emily will be like brother and sister. Those child catcher folks are still around, though, so I want you to be careful."

"I never had a brother before," said Emily, going back to the table as the pinging sound grew fainter and fainter. The rain began to lighten up too.

"And if I had a sister, I never knew her," said Jackson.

"So brother and sister it is, and I hope you will treat each other kindly, the way families were meant to do," Aunt Hilda told them.

As she was taking their dishes to the sink, she stopped and stared out the window. "Hmm," she said. "I don't much like the look of that sky."

"Why? What's the matter with it?" asked Jackson. "The rain's almost stopped."

"I don't see that yellow very often, and when I do . . ." Aunt Hilda took off her apron and went outside, Emily and Jackson close behind her.

The air was very still, as though the rain had gone and taken the wind with it. But the sky overhead did have a peculiar yellow look. When they turned around and stared out across the fields, they saw a huge dark cloud coming their way, and the big black cloud had a tail that whirled this way and that.

"Land sakes, it's a tornado!" Aunt Hilda said as the chickens scurried for cover. Spook whined, his tail between his legs, ears back, and Jackson's cap went sailing out over the yard. He had to run to catch it.

Far out in the south pasture, Emily could see that the sheep had clustered together, one big ball of wool, backs toward the wind. There was no telling where the cows were now. Aunt Hilda had put them in the sheep pasture till she could repair the fence. Old Billy was in the barn, still resting from the long journey of the morning.

The cloud was coming faster now, and the wind was becoming a gale.

"Rufus!" Emily cried. "I've got to get my turtle!"

But Aunt Hilda yanked her arm, pulling her toward the back of the house. "There's no time to get your turtle, Emily," she said. "Get in the storm cellar quickly." She dragged the two children through the blowing dust and dirt and lifted the heavy door of the storm cellar, which lay almost flat against the ground.

There was a short set of steps beneath it.

"Hurry, dears, hurry!" the big woman was saying as Jackson went stumbling on ahead of them, carrying the frightened dog. Soon they were at the bottom and the wind blew the door closed above them with a bang.

There was just enough light coming through the crack for Emily to make out a bench, but that was all. They were in a tiny room carved out of the earth, with the door for a roof.

Aunt Hilda sat down on the bench and pulled the children to her. "We'll be safe here," she said. "But we won't know about the house and barn till it's over."

Suddenly there was a roar that sounded more like a freight train than wind. It grew louder and louder till it pounded over them, while Emily screamed and Jackson covered his ears.

There was thumping and bumping, squawking and squeaking, baaing and neighing right outside the cellar. Suddenly, they heard a loud

KA-THUMP!

And what in wimpy waffles do you think it was?

TEN
Topsy-Turvy

Neither Jackson nor Emily nor Aunt Hilda could tell what the *ka-thump* was, because even though the tornado had moved on, they couldn't get the door above them to open.

Something must have been on top of it. Even the little sliver of daylight coming through the crack had disappeared.

"Land sakes, what do you suppose is out there?" Aunt Hilda said.

"Maybe a big old tree fell on us," said Jackson.

"There aren't any big trees near our house," said Aunt Hilda.

"Maybe the tornado blew the barn over on us," said Emily, hoping it wasn't true.

"We'll never know till we get out," said her aunt. "Here, you two, let's all push together and see if we can get the door to lift up."

They felt around in the darkness for each other's hands, until all six hands were touching the door above them.

"One . . . two . . . three . . . *push!*" said Aunt Hilda.

They pushed and grunted and puffed and pushed some more, but the door wouldn't budge.

"Let's try again," said Aunt Hilda.

Moving together in the darkness, they pushed hard on the count of three. Something above them moved, and they heard it sliding to the ground outside. When the door of the storm cellar flew open at last, there stood Clarabelle, looking down at them with straw between her horns and her eyes as big as saucers.

"Well, for goodness' sake, look what the wind blew

over!" Aunt Hilda said, stroking the frightened cow to calm her. "What happened, Clarabelle? That tornado just pick you up out of the pasture and set you down here?"

She checked the cow from the tip of her big nose to the tip of her long tail. "Well, I don't see a thing broken or where it ought not to be," she said, and patted the animal affectionately. "We've come through a lot together, haven't we, old girl?"

"Moo," said Clarabelle, testing each of her legs before she wandered off in search of her sister cow.

Emily, Jackson, and Aunt Hilda stood looking around. The land seemed all topsy-turvy, because even though the house and barn were still standing, part of the fence had blown down in the south pasture, and sheep were wandering about in confusion. Most of the chickens had lost some feathers. The beehive was upside down, the roof of the shed had blown into the horse trough, and everywhere Emily looked there were pieces of board and rags and tin and straw. All she could think about was Rufus, however, and when

she found him in the corner of his pen, clinging to the
wire along one side, she cupped him in her hands and
kissed his tiny head.

Aunt Hilda set to examining her little piece of land and gave a man-sized sigh. "Looks like I got me a mess of work here to do. Sure wish I had my Sam with me now."

"You got me!" said Jackson. He stood with his cap tipped back off his forehead, his green eyes fixed on Aunt Hilda. "Just tell me where to start."

Aunt Hilda looked down at the boy. "Thank you, Jackson," she said. "Of course you can help. I don't know what I'd do without you."

"And me!" said Emily. "I'll help too."

"How about the two of you herding all the sheep back to the south pasture? Spook will help. I'll set to work stringing the fence wire and nailing it to the posts. Every time I give a whistle, you come hold up a post for me," Aunt Hilda said.

And so, bit by bit, the things that were topsy-turvy were set right again. The children knew it would be weeks before everything was back the way it was before, but with a roof over their heads and food in the cupboard, Aunt Hilda told them, they were going to be fine.

• • •

It was a week later when Aunt Hilda found the time to get on Old Billy and head over to the judge's place. She wanted to find out how to go about becoming Jackson's legal guardian.

"There are some things you two could do to help while I'm gone," she said. "Take the wash off the line when it's dry, feed the chickens, collect the eggs, and mop the kitchen floor. I expect that'll keep you out of mischief till I get back."

Jackson was so excited at the thought of becoming part of the family that he jumped onto the swing. He pumped himself so high that Emily was afraid he'd swing right over the top of the branch.

"Let's get the chores done," she called after Aunt Hilda had gone down the road. "Which of them is the worst?"

"Mopping the floor," Jackson told her, slowing the swing down.

"Then that's what we'll do first, and it'll make all the rest seem easy," Emily said.

When the floor was shiny clean, they fed the chickens and collected the eggs—in a basket this time. Then they went outdoors to get the dry sheets and shirts off the clothesline.

They were just folding the wash when Spook suddenly pricked up his ears and gave a low growl.

Now, what in a turtle's toothache made the dog growl like that?

ELEVEN

The Man
in the Gray Suit

Aunt Hilda had left the gate open when she
went out that morning on horseback. And
what should come riding through it but a gray carriage
pulled by a gray horse?

Emily knew she was no longer in danger herself,
because Aunt Hilda was her guardian now. But . . .

"Jackson!" she cried. "Hide!"

She did not have to wait until the carriage got all
the way up to the house to know that the words on the
door read:

CATCHUM CHILD-CATCHING SERVICES, REDBUD DIVISION.

And she wasn't surprised when the carriage pulled up beside the cottage and a man in a gray suit held out a bunch of papers and said, "I'm looking for a boy named Jackson. I'm told he's been staying at this place."

"He's not here," said Emily, meaning the spot where she was standing, for it was quite true that Jackson was nowhere in sight.

"Where is he, then?" asked the man, stepping down and adjusting the tall gray hat on his head. Spook growled some more.

"I don't know," said Emily, which was also true, because she did not know just where Jackson was hiding.

"Then by the authority of the registrar of the first office of the ninth court of the twelfth district of the territory, I shall just look around," the gray man said, and he walked straight to the house, opened the door, and went inside.

Now, that made Emily mad. "It's not polite to walk

in someone's house without knocking," she told him.

"Catchum child catchers do not have to knock," he said. "If we had to knock first, we would never catch anyone." He pushed his glasses up higher on his nose and looked around the kitchen—under the table and inside the cupboards. He went into Emily's little bedroom next and checked under the bed, then went into Aunt Hilda's room. He peered into the closet there as well. Finally he went into the parlor.

"Aha!" he cried when he saw the little ladder that led to the loft, and at once he began to climb.

Emily's heart began to pound, for that was the very place she expected Jackson to be.

"Oho!" cried the man again when he reached the top. "And whose britches are these, may I ask? Whose socks and suspenders?"

And without waiting for an answer, he climbed down again and went straight to the door. Outside, he walked all around the house, Spook barking at his heels and Emily following close behind. This time he noticed the door to the storm cellar.

"Hey, hey!" he cried. He slid open the metal latch

and lifted the heavy door. Emily closed her eyes, unable to watch what would happen when he pulled Jackson out. But there was no boy hiding in the storm cellar, and the gray man moved to the shed and the springhouse, then on to the barn.

"Hee, hee!" the man cried when he saw the big stack of hay in one corner. He took a pitchfork and began stabbing at the pile—first here, then there—waiting for the yell that would tell him he had pricked a hiding boy.

But there was no Jackson in the haymow, and by this time even Emily was surprised. The man in the gray suit was angry. There were no "ahas" or "ohos" or "hee, hees" coming from him now.

"You know and I know that the young rascal Jackson has been staying here, and he is the property of Catchum Child Catchers, Incorporated," he said crossly to Emily.

"He isn't the property of anyone," Emily said boldly. "He is a free person and should be able to live with people who love him."

"Wrong!" said the man. "Until he is eighteen years

old, he is a ward of the territory, and we have been hired to deliver him to someone out west."

He began walking along the path near the garden now, his head turning right, then left, his sharp eyes looking for anything that moved. Emily walked along behind him, hoping that Jackson would stay put, wherever he was.

She was curious as to where Jackson could possibly be. She looked all around—the yard, the swing, the tree. She even looked high in the branches, expecting to see Jackson perched up there. No Jackson, of course. He wouldn't have had time to climb the tree before the man's carriage had entered the yard.

There was nothing in the garden but what should have been there: Aunt Hilda's bean plants in neat little rows, the knee-high corn, the tomato plants, the turnips, the scarecrow Aunt Hilda had made out of Sam's old clothes, and . . .

Suddenly Emily blinked and looked again.

What in the creakin' corncrib did she see?

TWELVE

Hiding

There were *two* scarecrows. When had there been *two* in Aunt Hilda's garden? Emily wondered.

One was wearing Sam's old pants and jacket, with a ragged straw hat on its cotton-ball head, and a post up its back. A crow flew down and landed on its head.

The other was shorter. It had a cap pulled down over its face, and was dressed in one of Aunt Hilda's freshly washed shirts, which hung down below its knees. The sleeves were so long that they flopped back and forth in the breeze, and there was no post holding it up. But just like the first one, this scarecrow stood perfectly still, its arms straight out at its sides.

Emily's heart leaped to her throat, and she put one hand over her mouth to stop the *Oh!* that was about to escape.

"He's got to be here somewhere," the man in the gray suit was saying. "I'll stay here till midnight if I have to, because when I leave, that boy's coming with me."

How long could Jackson stand out in the garden without moving? Emily wondered. How long could he keep his arms straight out at his sides? How still could he stand if a crow flew down and landed on *his* head?

Suddenly the gray man stopped.

"Now, that is odd indeed," he said, staring at the scarecrows.

"What is?" Emily asked in a tiny little voice.

"That crow, sitting on that scarecrow's head," said the man. "Doesn't seem like those scarecrows do much good in your aunt's garden."

"I . . . I guess not," said Emily.

Just then, Spook left Emily's side and went running

through the garden. Through the bean plants and across the turnips, right over to Jackson, who stood still as a wall in Aunt Hilda's clean shirt.

Spook snuffled about, wagging his tail, and the gray man said, "Aha!"

And when Jackson still didn't move, Spook jumped up, put his paws on Jackson's chest, and knocked him over backward.

"Oho! Hey, hey! Hee, hee!" cried the man in the gray suit, starting toward him. "I've got you now, you rascal!"

"Run, Jackson, run!" Emily cried, for the gray man's legs were twice as long as Jackson's.

Emily could not bear to watch. She covered her eyes, and when she peeped out, the man in the gray suit had Jackson by the arm and was dragging him toward the carriage. Spook ran alongside, frantically barking and growling.

"Let him go!" Emily screamed. "No! No!"

At that very moment, there was the *clippity-clop* of a horse's hooves coming through the gate at the end of the lane. Jackson was still struggling to get loose when Aunt Hilda rode through the gate and up to the house.

"Now, what's all this?" she asked. "What are you doing with my child?"

"He's not yours," said the gray man, waving his papers. "This boy is headed west, and he'll be on the next stagecoach coming through."

"I won't! I won't!" Jackson bellowed, trying to get away. "I want to stay here."

"Let that boy go!" Aunt Hilda demanded, getting down off Old Billy. "I just came from the judge, and

I have the papers to become his legal guardian. Once he signs his name, he's part of my family."

"But he hasn't signed them yet, and he won't!" the gray man said. "The Catchum Child-Catching Services has the authority to seize him. You're too late." And he opened the carriage door.

"He's *my* ward, and I aim to keep him here," Aunt Hilda argued.

At that moment, Jackson wriggled out of the oversized shirt he was wearing and rushed across the yard into Aunt Hilda's big arms, leaving the gray man holding nothing more than a shirtsleeve.

Aunt Hilda hustled Jackson into the house to sign the papers, and Spook stood guard at the door, snapping at the gray man's ankles when he tried to enter.

"Done!" Aunt Hilda said when she and Jackson appeared in the doorway. Jackson was beaming, and Aunt Hilda waved the papers in her hand with his signature on them, the ink not yet dry.

"Hooray!" cried Emily as the angry man in the gray suit climbed back into his gray carriage, growling. Even his growl sounded gray.

And what in a duck's dimple do you think happened next?

THIRTEEN

Down by the Gate

Why, they had a party, of course! Aunt Hilda baked a cake, and after supper they popped corn and played Hide-the-Thimble, and then Aunt Hilda took out Sam's old fiddle and played a tune while Emily danced and made Jackson laugh.

Aunt Hilda didn't play very well. In fact, her playing was rather awful, and Spook whined for her to stop. But it was such a wonderful evening that even bad music sounded good to Emily. Now that Jackson would be her brother, there was no telling what adventure they might have next.

• • •

The days that followed were busy ones, for there was still a lot of work to be done because of the tornado.

Emily found a small red wagon in the shed, and she and Jackson pulled it around the yard, picking up all the sticks and straw that were scattered about the place. Jackson climbed up on a ladder and nailed a piece of roof back onto the shed.

The next time Aunt Hilda went to town, she had many things to buy—more tin for the shed, more feed for the horse, more nails, more flour, more sugar and salt. Emily's bedroom needed curtains, and Jackson would want another blanket soon.

"I'll be gone all day," Aunt Hilda told them. "Please wash the breakfast dishes. Pick the last of the peaches and put them in a basket. Feed the chickens, sweep the floor, and pull the weeds in my flower garden."

Emily and Jackson promised they would, and as soon as Aunt Hilda and Old Billy disappeared out the gate, the children set to work washing the breakfast dishes and putting them back in the cupboard.

They did all the work they'd been told to do, and when they were done, they even picked some flowers and put them in a vase on the table so that the kitchen would be bright and cheerful when Aunt Hilda came back.

Later, as they were sailing paper boats in the creek, Emily thought she heard a noise.

"Listen!" she said.

Jackson straightened up and listened.

"It sounds like a cow mooing," he said.

"I don't think so," said Emily. "It sounds like a dove cooing."

They listened some more.

"It sounds like the wind moaning," said Jackson.

"It sounds like somebody groaning," said Emily.

They waded out of the water and put on their socks and shoes. The strange sound seemed to be coming from the end of the lane. Spook heard it too, because he pricked up his ears and led the way toward the road.

Up ahead, Emily saw something black near the gate.

"What's that?" she asked, pointing. "It looks like a heap of old rags."

"It looks like a pile of dirt," said Jackson.

And then the pile moved. A hand reached out and clutched at the gate, and a low moan made the hair on Spook's back stand on end.

"It's a *person!*" cried Emily, beginning to run. "I think someone needs help."

When she reached the fence, she opened the gate and knelt down beside a woman dressed all in black. The woman wore a black hat on her head and a black veil over her face. Her black dress had a high collar, and there were black stockings and black shoes on her feet, black gloves on her hands. She was holding a tin cup with a few pennies in it.

The widow woman Aunt Hilda told us about! Emily thought.

"What's the matter?" she asked the woman kindly. "Can we help?"

"W . . . water!" the widow said in a low, sad voice. "Please, my dear, may I have some water?"

"Of course!" said Emily. "We'll bring some."

"I'm so tired," the widow said then. "If I just had a place to lie down . . ."

Emily looked at Jackson and then at the poor woman.

Now, what in steamin' stompers would they do?

FOURTEEN

The Widow Woman

The kind thing to do, the children decided, was to take the poor woman to their cottage and let her lie down and rest. That was what Aunt Hilda would do. But how could they get her there?

"Can you walk?" Jackson asked her.

"I'm so very tired," the woman repeated. "Too, too tired."

"We could pull her in the wagon," Emily suggested.

"We'll be back," said Jackson. "We'll get you to the house."

So off they went, back up the lane.

"I don't know, she's awful big," Jackson said. "Do you suppose she'll fit?"

"We have to try," said Emily. "And if she's thirsty, she might be hungry too. She'll probably eat a lot. We could give her the beans and muffins Aunt Hilda left for us."

Jackson wasn't eager to give up his lunch, but there were other things in the cupboard he could have, so he figured he could be generous too. "And milk," he said. "We could give her a tall glass of cold milk."

Inside the cottage, Emily filled a jar with water from the water bucket. And with Jackson pulling the little red wagon, they went back down the long lane to the road.

The widow was sitting up when they got there and reached out one gloved hand for the water jar. She held it to her lips beneath her black veil, then gulped the water down so fast that it made little glugging sounds in her throat.

"Do you think you can get in the wagon?" Jackson asked her.

"If I have help, dearie," the woman said, and holding on to the gate for balance, she pulled herself up off the ground. Jackson and Emily pushed the wagon beneath her. The woman sat down with a plop.

She was a very tall woman, with large feet. She sat with her legs hanging over either side of the wagon, her heavy boots scraping the road now and then as they moved along. Emily wondered if the wagon would break. Jackson pulled and Emily pushed, and finally they got the wagon up to the cottage door and helped the woman out.

"You are so kind, dearies," the woman said. "Your parents certainly have raised you to be good children."

"We live with my aunt Hilda," Emily told her. "She's in town today, but she'll be back this afternoon."

"Well, I'm sure she wouldn't mind if I rest here for a bit, " the woman said, fanning herself with her black pocketbook. "I do feel faint. If I could just lie down awhile . . ."

Emily wondered where to put her. Her own little bed was much too small, and surely the woman couldn't climb the ladder to Jackson's loft. The only thing to do was take her to Aunt Hilda's large bed. So that was what Emily did.

The woman in black thanked her and sat down. Her black veil fluttered back and forth across her face as she continued to fan herself.

"Would you like to take off your hat and cool your head?" asked Emily politely.

At that, the woman began to cry. "Oh, no indeed," she wept. "These are the clothes I wore to my husband's funeral, and I must wear them for a year to honor him."

It seemed strange to Emily that a widow had to sleep in her hat and boots to honor her dead husband. But she told the woman to get some rest, and that when she felt strong enough to walk to the table, they would give her a little lunch before she went on her way.

"Thank you," the woman said. "I will never forget your kindness."

Emily went back out and closed the door, but not quite all the way. She and Jackson prepared a lunch for the widow—a plate of beans, two corn muffins, and a ripe tomato.

Then Jackson remembered the milk. He went to the springhouse, where Aunt Hilda kept her milk and butter and eggs. He lifted the jug of milk from the cold water and poured some into a pitcher. Then he carefully carried the pitcher back to the cottage and set it on the table. The lunch looked so good that it was hard for the children not to eat it themselves, but they made do with crackers and cheese and a small shriveled apple they found in the cupboard.

After some time had passed and the woman had not come out of the bedroom, Emily went to the door and listened. She didn't hear a sound, but she was afraid to knock for fear the widow woman was sleeping. So she silently pushed the door open just a little more to peep inside. The bed was empty.

Now, where in the gooey guppies could the widow have been?

FIFTEEN
In the Kitchen

The widow woman was on her knees, her head almost touching the floor. One arm was *under* the bed.

"Oh!" said Emily. "Have you lost something?"

The widow woman sat up quickly. "You startled me," she said in her low, sad voice. "I was praying."

"Oh," Emily said again. "Well, we made some lunch for you. I can help you to the kitchen."

"You are so kind, so kind," the woman said, but she got to her feet sooner than Emily thought she would be able to. Both Emily and Jackson were happy to see that the rest had made her stronger.

"My, doesn't this look good," the widow woman said as she sat down in a chair.

She placed her long arms on the table but did not take her black gloves off, even to eat. When she ate, she took large forkfuls of beans, Emily noticed, not dainty little bites. She must have been hungry indeed!

Jackson and Emily nibbled cheese and crackers as they watched their lunch disappearing behind the heavy black veil.

"I suppose," said the widow, "that it's hard for your aunt to make a living way out here, so far from town."

"Oh, she does all right," said Jackson. "She raises sheep and chickens."

"Lucky, lucky woman," said the widow, and stuffed half a corn muffin in her mouth. "Not like me. I just live from pillar to post, wherever I can find a bed. The only money I have in this world is what I collect in my tin cup, and that's precious little."

When the children said nothing, the woman continued: "Still, I suppose there are many expenses when you run a sheep farm, and if the roof went tomorrow, your poor aunt wouldn't have a penny to replace it."

Jackson chuckled. "She could replace it, all right. Could buy herself a hundred roofs if she had to." Emily kicked him under the table, knowing that Aunt Hilda didn't like the children to brag about their money. Jackson coughed and reached for another cracker.

"We were lucky when the tornado hit that it didn't do more damage than it did," said Emily quickly.

"My, yes," said the woman in black. "I was huddled in a ditch when that twister came by, praying that it would take me and let me join my dear departed husband, so sad has my life become." She sniffled a little and dabbed at her eyes beneath the veil.

When she straightened up, she said, "I don't suppose you could spare a poor widow woman a few dollars to speed her on her way?"

Emily and Jackson looked at each other uneasily. They had no dollars lying around, because they never needed any; there was no place close by to spend them. The only way for them to get a few dollars was to move the big rock and dig up the wooden box with the coffee tin inside it. And they would never, ever do that in front of a stranger.

"I'm afraid we can't," said Emily. "Aunt Hilda takes care of the money."

The widow nodded sadly. "Yes, yes, of course. But . . . what if something should happen to your dear sweet aunt? I mean, an accident with her horse and wagon, perhaps. Surely you must know where she keeps *some* of her money, or how would the two of you survive?"

Emily was beginning to feel very uncomfortable now. Her mother had died in a horse-and-carriage accident, which was why she had come to live with Aunt Hilda in the first place. Jackson looked wary too.

"The bank would take care of us," he said.

"Ah! The bank, is it? Your aunt Hilda must be a very wealthy woman indeed if she has enough money to put in a bank," said the widow, her voice a bit louder still.

But then she dabbed at her eyes again beneath her veil and sighed. "Well, my dears, I must be on my way, for I have a long, sad road ahead. Do you think you could possibly give me some privacy so I can wash up a little here at the sink before I go? I'm so dusty."

"Of course," said Emily, glad to hear that the woman was leaving. She got a towel and put the washbasin in the sink along with a bar of soap. Then she and Jackson went into the parlor, closing the kitchen door behind them. They sat on the sofa listening to the pump handle going up and down, and water splashing into the basin.

"I don't trust her," Jackson said finally. "She asks too many questions."

"She'll be gone soon," said Emily. "At least we gave her our lunch. Aunt Hilda will say that was the kind thing to do."

They sat waiting some more, listening. The splashing of water had stopped, and the house was absolutely quiet. Finally Jackson got up, tiptoed to the door of the kitchen, and opened it just a crack.

"Jackson!" Emily whispered, shocked. Did this boy have no manners at all, to peep in on a woman who was washing up?

But a moment later he turned to Emily, and his eyes were huge.

"Emily!" he whispered, and motioned her over, one finger to his lips.

What in shootin' shivers did he see?

SIXTEEN

Oh, No!

Emily tiptoed to the kitchen door and peeked through the crack. There was the tall widow woman, standing at the washbasin with the towel in her hands. The hat was still on her head and the veil was still over her face, but she wasn't wearing her gloves, and her sleeves were rolled up to her shoulders.

And there, on one big arm, was a tiger tattoo!

Emily almost screamed but caught herself in time, for Jackson was pulling her off into a corner.

"Jackson!" she whispered, her voice trembling.

"It's Uncle Victor! What are we going to do?"

"Shhh!" Jackson said. "Don't let him find out we know."

"What do you mean?" Emily whispered back. "We know exactly why he's here. If he can't get my ten million dollars one way, he'll get it another. He just wanted to search the house."

Jackson nodded. "He knows your aunt's smart enough to keep your money in a bank, but he figures we're hiding some of it here, and he aims to find it."

"And if he's been hanging around town in widow's clothing, he knows just what days Aunt Hilda goes to market, and that's when he came out here," said Emily.

They sneaked back to the crack in the doorway and peeked into the kitchen again. Noiselessly, Uncle Victor was opening cupboard doors, one after another, searching each shelf, digging his big hand into a spare pitcher and poking his finger into the sugar bowl. Then he checked the flour bin—which was easy, because it was almost empty.

"What we need to do," Jackson told Emily, "is play

along. Act like we don't know who he is. It'll go better for us."

But Emily wasn't so sure. She knew now that Uncle Victor had been searching under Aunt Hilda's bed, looking for money. He had probably checked under the mattress and gone through all her dresser drawers as well. And what if he got it in his mind to take Emily's little turtle, Rufus, and threaten to kill him unless she told where the money was hidden?

"I've got to get Rufus, just in case," she told Jackson, and slipped out the parlor door.

Emily hurried around the house to the little pen she had made for her turtle. She remembered how Uncle Victor had tricked her once before by threatening to kill her turtle if she didn't obey. She wasn't going to take any chances. Emily picked Rufus up and slipped him deep in her apron pocket.

"You'll be safe here," she whispered. How she wished that Aunt Hilda were home!

Should she even go back in the house? she wondered. How long could Uncle Victor go on pretending he was a widow woman and being nice? Maybe they should run and hide while they could. She slipped back inside to suggest it to Jackson, but he wasn't there. Perhaps he had already run away, and she was alone with the person she disliked most in the whole wide world.

Jackson must have gone out looking for her, but after a while he came back and sat down beside her on the parlor sofa. A minute later, Uncle Victor came out of the kitchen. The sleeves of the dress were rolled down again and the gloves were back on his hands.

"I feel so much better after my little rest," he told the children in his woman's voice. Goose bumps rose on Emily's arms just hearing it, now that she knew who it belonged to. "You were so kind to give me lunch. Do you think I could have a little tour before I leave? I would love to look around this charming place."

"I . . . I think it would be better if Aunt Hilda were here," Emily said.

"Just a little walk," Uncle Victor said. "I'm sure your aunt Hilda wouldn't mind, now that you've brought me this far."

"Sure," said Jackson. "Step right this way."

Was Jackson crazy? Emily wondered. Did he really think he could outwit the man with the eyes of a weasel, the growl of a bear, and the tiger tattoo on his arm?

What in the dabble dooby did Jackson have in mind?

SEVENTEEN
Beneath the Veil

Emily followed Jackson and Uncle Victor, her heart going *thumpa-thumpa-thumpa* all the while.

The only reason the "widow woman" wanted to walk around the property was to look for places Aunt Hilda might be hiding her money, Emily knew. What if he guessed?

"Such a beautiful day!" said Uncle Victor in his womanly voice. He was more lively now. "It makes me feel young again."

"Then I'll bet you'd like the creek," Jackson told him. "That's where Emily and I go to catch crawdads."

He led Uncle Victor to the very back of the yard, where a bit of the creek flowed through. It was here that they had built a dam out of rocks to make their wading hole a little deeper, and a bridge of stepping-stones to get to the other side.

Something looked different, however. The dry white tops of the stones that led from one bank to the other had disappeared; it looked as though someone had turned each stone upside down. Instead of a nice dry top sticking above the water, each stone was covered with shiny green moss.

"I know you'll want to see our cows out there," Jackson said to Uncle Victor, pointing to the pasture, and motioned for the "widow woman" to go across.

Uncle Victor picked up his skirts and put one big foot on the first stone. But the minute he stepped forward onto the next one, his foot slipped out from under him and down he went in the water, his black dress soaked to the waist. Emily watched in horror.

The cry that came out of Uncle Victor's mouth

sounded first like that of a man, but it quickly changed to "Goodness gracious!" and Uncle Victor picked himself up.

"Oh! Let me help you," Jackson said, reaching out one hand.

But Uncle Victor said, "I don't think I want to see the cows. I'm a lady not used to creeks and such. Why don't we keep to the yard?"

Thumpa-thumpa-thumpa went Emily's heart, but she heard herself saying, "I think you would like Aunt Hilda's flower garden, then. Ladies always like to walk through the garden."

Uncle Victor was trying to squeeze the water out of his skirt as they walked along. "Yes, yes," he said. "Let's see the garden."

Aunt Hilda was very proud of her flowers, Emily knew. It was a big garden, with petunias on one side and geraniums on the other and lots of roses in between.

Jackson took right over. "Ladies first," he said, and directed Uncle Victor down the very middle of the garden, on a path with rosebushes on either side. The branches reached out, almost touching each other, and as Uncle Victor walked deeper into the garden, his long black dress caught on the thorns. When he tried to get the dress free, they pricked right through the black gloves on his big hands.

Now the howl was a man's howl indeed, but Uncle Victor recovered enough to say, "Drat those flowers! I don't think I want to see any more."

"So sorry," said Jackson. "You need a little rest before you go on your way, Widow Woman. Come sit on the swing. Ladies always like a turn on the swing. And the breeze will help dry your dress."

Uncle Victor seemed to be growling under his breath, Emily could tell. But he followed them across the yard to the big tree. When he sat down on the board swing, the branch sank low, and his big feet dragged on the ground.

"We'll both push," said Jackson, and together he and Emily pushed Uncle Victor higher and higher until the skirt of the black dress blew up almost over his head and his big hairy legs showed above the tops of his stockings.

"Stop! Stop!" he bellowed, trying to hold the dress down with one hand and keep the hat and veil on with the other.

But the next time he sailed forward, the hat with the veil flew right off, and with a roar, Uncle Victor sprang from the swing and went flying to the ground, his boots making a loud thud as he landed. And when he turned to face the children, he wasn't playing "widow woman" any longer.

Was this the rabble-scrabble end of the road for Emily and Jackson?

EIGHTEEN

The Eyes of a Weasel

"**U**ncle Victor!" Emily cried, only pretending to be surprised. But she didn't have to pretend to be scared. She could feel her legs shaking.

"Okay, you miserable little wretches, you listen to me!" roared her uncle. "I'm through being nice. I want to know where Hilda hides her money, and don't tell me it's in the bank. Nobody keeps *all* her money in a bank. Now where is it?"

And when neither of the children answered, Victor strode across the yard, the wet black dress making smacking noises against his legs, and grabbed Jackson by one ear. Jackson yelped in pain. Spook growled and nipped at Uncle Victor's ankle, but the man with the tiger tattoo only kicked him away.

"Where *is* it?" Uncle Victor bellowed, and he sounded like a whole jungle full of lions, all roaring at the same time.

"It's . . . it's . . . in a coffee tin," Jackson said, wincing in pain.

Emily gasped. "Jackson! No!" she whispered.

"*Show* me!" Victor yelled, and when he let go of the boy's ear, Jackson started toward the big rock in the middle of the yard.

But he didn't stop at the rock. He went on over to the cottage and pointed to the porch steps. "Under there," he said.

Uncle Victor pushed him aside and got down on his knees in the black dress. He reached around under the steps.

"I don't feel any coffee tin," he said.

"A little more to the right," said Jackson.

"Where? Where?"

"A little farther," said Jackson.

Uncle Victor stretched his arm in as far as it would go and suddenly there was a loud snap. The man with the tiger tattoo howled with pain and pulled his arm out. There was a rattrap fastened to his fingers, and he flung his arm this way and that until the trap fell off.

"You good-for-nothing scalawags!" Victor cried, and reached out to box Jackson's ears.

But Jackson ducked and said, "Okay, maybe it's not under there. I think I heard her say it was in the barn beneath the hay."

"Show me where!" Uncle Victor demanded, and again Jackson led the way, Uncle Victor and Emily close behind, with Spook growling at Victor's heels. With every step, Emily felt more and more frightened. Uncle Victor would be very angry if Jackson tricked him again, and she knew the money was not under the hay.

They walked into the big dark opening of the barn, and Jackson pointed to the haystack. "Somewhere under there," he said.

Uncle Victor rushed greedily toward the big stack

of hay in one corner. He grabbed an armful and threw it over his shoulder. Then another and another.

But on his fourth grab, he suddenly gave a big "Yeow!" and sprang backward. It was then that Emily saw the sharp ends of a pitchfork someone had hidden under the hay, and there were prick marks along the arm with the tiger tattoo.

Uncle Victor was furious. He whirled around to strike Jackson, but this time Emily stepped forward.

"Don't hurt him," she said. "I'll tell you where Aunt Hilda keeps the money. In a wooden box."

"Emily, no!" whispered Jackson. "Don't tell."

"Where?" bellowed her uncle. "Don't waste my time or you'll be sorry!"

Emily led the way out of the barn and pointed in the direction of the big rock, but her eyes looked beyond it, and Uncle Victor went where she was pointing. He walked right over to a large wooden box sitting on a bench and opened the lid.

Instantly a dozen bees flew out, and then a dozen more.

"A beehive!" roared Uncle Victor, but the children

were already running up onto the porch and into the cottage. With a bee on his back and another on his neck, Uncle Victor swatted at them as he ran, and charged into the house behind Emily and Jackson.

But they had already reached the parlor and quickly climbed up the ladder to Jackson's loft. By the time Uncle Victor swatted off the last bee and reached the parlor, Jackson had pulled the ladder up after them.

The man with the tiger tattoo stood on the rug below, his weasel eyes flashing, his sharp teeth grinding, his fists clenched. A low growl came from his throat.

"I want that money before your aunt Hilda gets home," he said. "And you're going to tell me where it is. If you don't . . ."

"Yeah, what?" Jackson taunted.

"If you don't, then first, I'll take an ax to Hilda's parlor. I'll smash the sofa, smash the chair, smash the windows . . ." His eyes went from one piece of furniture to the next, and Emily was afraid he would notice the drawer of the lamp table with the gold watch inside. He would certainly take that watch if he found it. "And after I smash the parlor to pieces," Uncle Victor continued with a cruel smile, "I'll pull that big old table in from the kitchen, I'll climb up on top of it, and I'll start smashing *you!*"

Emily couldn't bear to imagine anyone smashing Aunt Hilda's cottage to pieces, but she knew that Uncle Victor was just mean enough to do it. And she had to get him away from the lamp table. With her uncle shouting and Spook barking, she could hardly think what to do.

She swung her legs over the edge of the loft and looked down at her uncle. "Okay," she said. "I'll tell."

And what in a toad's toenail did she tell him?

NINETEEN

Emily Talks

"The money is in a tin can in a wood box buried in the ground," Emily said.

"Emily!" Jackson cried, his eyes huge. "We were never supposed to tell!"

"Aha!" said Uncle Victor. "Now you're getting smart. Get down here, you musty maggots, and show me where to dig."

"Emily, we *promised*!" Jackson pleaded.

Emily said nothing. As Jackson lowered the ladder and Emily climbed down, he came after her, still whispering, "No, Emily, no!"

She led the procession outside and around the house to the storm cellar. She reached down and opened the heavy door.

"Down there?" Uncle Victor asked, puzzled.

"It's a dirt floor," she told him.

"Well, that Hilda's a sly one, I'll say that!" Uncle Victor told her. He grabbed a shovel that was leaning against the house and motioned for the children to go down first. "Show me where to dig, and stay out of my way," he said when they reached the bottom.

"Right there in the middle," said Emily.

"You'll have to dig pretty deep," said Jackson.

"And you'll have to dig fast if you want to reach it before Aunt Hilda gets back," said Emily.

"If she finds out we told you, we'll get the strap for sure," said Jackson. "We could get the hoe and spade and help."

"Well, get them, then," Uncle Victor growled. "But Emily stays here, in case you decide to run out on me." And he thrust the shovel into the hard-packed ground and began to dig.

Thumpa-thumpa-thumpa went Emily's heart as Jackson went back up the steps and out into the sunlight. She knew that Jackson was up to something, but she didn't know what. They lived too far out to go for help or to get to a neighbor's in time.

Pretty soon she could hear the clank of garden tools getting louder as Jackson returned from the barn. Uncle Victor was sweating in the long black dress as the pile of dirt beside him grew higher and higher and the hole deeper and deeper.

When Jackson got to the open door of the storm cellar, he called, "Coming down!"

But when Uncle Victor moved over to give Jackson room at the bottom of the steps, Emily rushed up them instead, and in a flash, the children banged the door of the storm cellar shut, then latched the metal lock.

When Uncle Victor roared from below, they sat down on top of the door, just to be on the safe side. Uncle Victor bellowed and cussed and banged against the door, but Emily and Jackson never budged.

If that wasn't the craziest noise they had ever heard: Uncle Victor roaring, Spook barking, the shovel banging, even the chickens starting to fret out in the henhouse.

Just at that moment Spook's barking turned to happy little yips. Far off down the lane, Aunt Hilda's wagon was rolling through the gate. Old Billy trotted with his head down, pulling the wagon full of things from the market.

"Hooray!" Emily and Jackson shouted, but they didn't get off the storm cellar door.

A few minutes later, Aunt Hilda pulled up beside the cottage. There was no sound at all from the cellar.

"What's all this?" she asked, looking at the two children sitting there on the cellar door, holding the spade and the hoe.

"Well," said Jackson, "it's been a wild day."

"How so?" asked Aunt Hilda.

"First of all, that widow woman you've seen in town was begging at our gate," Emily told her.

"Poor dear soul," Aunt Hilda said, getting down off the wagon. "I hope you gave her some water and something to eat."

"Oh, we brought her here to the house to rest up," said Jackson.

"I'm proud of you," said Aunt Hilda.

"Then we gave her some lunch," said Emily.

"That was a kind thing to do," said her aunt.

"Then we took her down to the creek and she fell in," said Jackson.

"What?" said Aunt Hilda, turning and staring at him.

"And we took her through the flower garden and the rosebushes tore her dress," said Emily.

Aunt Hilda gasped. "Why on earth . . . ?"

"And when we took her to the barn, she got stuck by a pitchfork," said Jackson.

"What a terrible thing to do to a poor widow woman!" cried Aunt Hilda. "What got into you children?"

"And now we've got her trapped here in the cellar and won't let her out till you say so," said Emily.

"Hilda!" bellowed Uncle Victor from the darkness beneath the door. "Get those blasted kids off this door and let me out."

"Victor!" cried Aunt Hilda. And then, to the children, she said, "Don't move."

She went into the house, and when she came out again, she had the fireplace poker in her hand.

"All right," she told Emily and Jackson. "Open it up."

When Uncle Victor came out in the wet black dress, his face was as red as a raspberry, and he was dripping sweat.

"Victor," Aunt Hilda said, "if you aren't the darnedest sight I've ever seen. You've got about one minute to get yourself down the lane, out the gate, and up the road before I take this poker to you. And if you ever set foot on my land again, you'll be sorry, don't think you won't." Then she looked down at the dog. "Show him out, Spook," she said.

This time Spook didn't just bark and nip. With a growl, he lunged at Uncle Victor's chest, and Uncle Victor took off at a run, holding his skirts up to keep from tripping. Spook was right on his heels, tearing at the dress. Aunt Hilda waited until Emily's uncle had reached the gate, and then she laughed so hard her shoulders shook.

Finally, when she had caught her breath, she said,

"Now, that is about the funniest thing I've seen since the rooster got his head stuck in a piece of watermelon. I hope his shirt and britches are hid somewhere close by. Without his hat and veil, he'd sure be a sight, wearing that dress all the way back into town."

Emily laughed a little too, but she asked, "What if Uncle Victor comes back?"

"Oh, I wouldn't worry," said her aunt. "I don't think he'll try that for a while."

But how in flyin' fishes could anybody know for sure?

TWENTY

In the Bag

Aunt Hilda was surely proud of her two young'uns.

"You did exactly the right thing," she told them again the next morning. "That old weasel Victor is lucky we didn't leave him in the storm cellar a day or two just to reflect on his own miserable self. After you finish your chores for the morning, you two run off and play. I won't need you again till supper."

So Jackson and Emily did just that. They swung on the swing and waded in the creek. And then, as the afternoon grew a little cooler, they decided to play hide-and-seek, and Jackson said he'd be it.

Emily loved hide-and-seek because there were so many wonderful places to hide on Aunt Hilda's land. While Jackson was counting to one hundred slowly by fives, Emily set off away from the house and barn, because some of the doors squeaked when they were opened, and that would give her hiding place away.

There was a big old elm tree deep in the woods with a grassy place beneath it—the perfect place to rest a bit and hide. She climbed the fence at the back of the yard and carefully made her way through the brush, trying not to break a twig or crunch dry leaves.

"Spook! Go home!" she whispered when she discovered the black dog tagging along after her, but he liked the game as well as anyone, especially the part where Jackson would shout, "I spy Emily!" and then everyone, including Spook, would race back to home base.

Emily had just about reached the elm tree when Spook suddenly stopped and growled. And at that very minute, Emily felt four big fingers and a thumb wrap themselves over her mouth from behind. The fingers belonged to a big old hand, the hand was attached to a big old arm, and on that arm was a tiger tattoo.

Spook snapped and growled at the tiger man, who rapidly taped Emily's mouth shut and tied her hands behind her back, despite her squirming and kicking. Spook kept barking and nipping while Uncle Victor stuffed her into a big burlap bag. Then there came a terrible yelp, and Emily cringed as she heard Uncle Victor's boot connect with the little dog.

"That should take care of you, you stupid mutt," Victor snarled, slinging the bag over his shoulder and setting off quickly. Emily kicked and squirmed some more, but it did no good, and now she was bouncing up and down, her arms and legs all squished together.

How long had Uncle Victor been hiding in the woods, waiting to grab her? she wondered. Where was he going, and why was he in such a hurry?

Spook was still barking, but from some distance behind them, not wanting another kick. After a while Emily heard her uncle panting and felt him slowing down. Finally he stopped completely and dropped the bag on the ground with a thump. Luckily, Emily landed on her bottom.

"If I had the time, I'd stop that fool dog's barking once and for all," he said. "I'm tired of waiting for that money, Emily Wiggins. You've got ten million dollars sitting in the bank, and I want some of it. While your aunt was out in the potato field this afternoon, I slipped a ransom note under her door. Told her if she ever expects to see you alive again, she'll turn over half that money to me."

Inside the burlap bag, Emily shivered. She knew that her aunt Hilda loved her so much she would give Uncle Victor *all* the money just to have Emily back again. And that was probably what Uncle Victor would demand. After he got half the money, he would say he'd changed his mind and wanted the whole ten million.

I'm not worried, she told herself. *Aunt Hilda will find me.*

But as if he could read her thoughts, Uncle Victor picked up the bag and slung it over his shoulder again. Then he said, "Where I'm taking you, she'll never think to look. And I told her in that note that if she tells the law, she'll never see you again."

Emily knew that he meant what he said. Uncle Victor had never liked children, especially not Emily. He was walking fast again now, as though in a great hurry. Where could he possibly be taking her, where Aunt Hilda would never look? Spook's barking and yipping seemed farther behind than ever.

Long after the barking had faded away, Emily sensed that her uncle was slowing down again, and then she heard another sound: somewhere a calliope was playing—that happy organlike instrument that made music on showboats traveling up and down the river.

There were no showboats where Aunt Hilda lived, however. The closest one was on the Cottonwood River, several miles away. Aunt Hilda had promised that sometime before the summer was over, she and Emily and Jackson would all pile into the wagon and go see a show. But that would never happen now.

The music grew louder and louder. *Thud, thud* went Uncle Victor's boots on some wooden planks.

What in the quakin', shakin' world was Uncle Victor going to do next?

TWENTY-ONE
Company

The burlap bag was swinging and swaying, back and forth, back and forth, and now it seemed to Emily that her uncle was going down a long flight of stairs. The calliope music grew fainter and the noise of an engine grew louder. Then Uncle Victor dropped the bag to the floor. Emily heard a door close, and knew they were probably in a room somewhere at the very bottom of a large boat.

The small opening at the top of the bag grew wider

and wider, and then Emily saw Uncle Victor's evil eyes peering down at her.

"Okay, you useless brat," Victor said. "Here's the deal. Your aunt should have read the ransom note by now. She has all day tomorrow to get the money out of the bank. Tonight the showboat travels downriver, playing its music and advertising its show, which will play back here at Cottonwood Junction tomorrow. The boat doesn't stop till it gets back here, so there's no chance for you to run off. If you're quiet and don't call out, I'll come in every so often to give you crackers and water."

Crackers and water? thought Emily. What about air to breathe? A chance to stretch her legs? A place to go to the bathroom?

Uncle Victor was talking again. "But in case you're thinking of getting loose and going for help, I'm telling the captain I'm a private inspector, assigned to capture some thievin' kids who have been hiding out on showboats and picking the pockets of the customers. Any kids they find aboard, they're to turn over to me. You get out of this bag and make any trouble, I'll catch you, put a weight in the bag with you, and drop you to the bottom of the river faster'n you can squeal.

So if you know what's good for you and you want to see your aunt Hilda again, you'll stay quiet and wait till she hands over the money. She knows just where to put it. I'll check that old hollow tree when the boat goes back upriver."

And with that, he pulled the cords at the top of the bag tight together again, and through the small round opening, Emily watched his fingers tying a big knot. At the same moment, the showboat whistle gave two toots, the engine noise grew louder, and the boat left the landing and was on its way down the Cottonwood River.

Emily heard the door open and close again, and then Uncle Victor was gone. The only noise left was the engine and the low whir of the paddlewheel as it propelled the boat through the water.

Thumpa-thumpa-thumpa went Emily's heart. Her hands were still tightly tied together behind her body, but she found that she had just enough room to twist and turn and wiggle and waggle to get one hand loose. Then it was easy to loosen the other hand and take the tape off her mouth.

The opening at the top of the burlap bag, however, was too small to get her arm through. Even if she yelled as loudly as she could, no one would hear above the noise of the engine, and they wouldn't believe her anyway, not with Uncle Victor telling his lies. No, Emily thought. She would stay right where she was for now and try to calm down so she could think what to do next.

Suddenly she heard the soft click of the door opening again, and wondered if Uncle Victor had come back. There was no sound of a man's footsteps on the floor, however. In fact, there were no footsteps at all, but something poked her gently on one side of the bag.

Emily froze. Was it someone who was curious about what was in the bag? Was one of the sailors about to discover her and turn her over to the captain? Something poked her again, and Emily heard muffled snuffles and pants and felt something climbing on top of the bag.

"Spook?" Emily whispered. "Oh, Spook! How did you get in here?"

Then she heard Jackson's loud whisper.

"Emily?" His face was close to the opening at the top of the bag. "We got on at the last minute and hid in a barrel outside the door when your uncle dumped you in here. He's gone to look for the captain, and I heard what he's going to tell him."

"Oh, Jackson! How did you know Uncle Victor got me?"

"I was still looking for you in the woods and heard Spook barking, so I figured he knew your hiding place. When I saw your uncle with that big bag over his shoulder and Spook barking at him, I figured it out pretty quick and followed him here."

"Can you get me out?" Emily asked.

"I'm working on the knot, but it's tight," Jackson said.

Just then, they heard heavy footsteps in the hall outside. Jackson grabbed Spook and covered his muzzle so he couldn't bark. The doorknob rattled and the door started to open, then stopped. Uncle Victor and the captain were talking right outside.

"Much obliged, Captain," Uncle Victor was saying. "I'll keep a sharp eye out for any lying, thieving children. If a certain girl's aboard, she's a crafty one. She's been known to steal a diamond right off a lady's finger."

"Come on up and have a drink with me in the pilothouse," the captain said. "It's a nice night out there, and we're glad to have you aboard."

"Indeed I will," Uncle Victor answered, and Emily and Jackson breathed easier as the door closed all the way and Uncle Victor and the captain went back down the hall.

"Listen, Emily," Jackson said as his fingers worked hard to untie the knot that held the bag closed. "We've got to get a message to Aunt Hilda. I heard Victor tell you he'd left a ransom note for her. Even if she somehow traced him to the river's edge, she'd never know where he went next. Victor must have known the showboat's schedule and had it all planned."

"We could jump overboard and swim to shore," Emily suggested.

Jackson shook his head. "Too dangerous. Someone would try to rescue us and we'd be turned right over to Uncle Victor."

"Can't you get that knot untied?" Emily asked, impatient to be let out.

"It's really tight," Jackson said as Spook poked his nose in the hole, making the job even more difficult.

"Where are we on the ship?" Emily asked as Jackson continued to work.

"Some kind of a dusty storeroom with a porthole. Some boxes, some supplies, and a pile of flyers advertising the next show," Jackson answered.

"If the boat would just stop someplace—*any*place— we could sneak off and find our way back home," Emily said. "Is it true that the boat will go down the river a ways and turn around, but won't stop till it's back at Cottonwood Junction?"

"It's true," said Jackson, "and that won't be till tomorrow. By then your aunt will have the money, and she'll turn it over to Victor the minute we land."

Suddenly Jackson's fingers stopped working at the knot. "Listen! I have an idea!"

This time he thrust his skinny hand through the small opening, twisting and turning it this way and that until he could reach Emily's hair.

"Ouch!" she said as he tugged at her ribbon.

"Sorry," he said. "I'm going to wrap this up in one of those flyers about the show, put it in Spook's mouth, tell him to go to Aunt Hilda, and drop him overboard. But I've got to hurry before we get too far away."

"But Jackson, can he make it?" Emily cried.

"He's a better swimmer than I am," Jackson said.

Emily heard paper being folded, and then Spook's panting as he took the paper in his mouth.

"Good dog! Good Spook!" Jackson said, and Emily heard the door open and close again as her friend went out. Then all was still.

Who in rushin' rapids knows what might happen next?

TWENTY-TWO
Hiding Out

Jackson came back to tell Emily that he had dropped Spook in the water at the boat's stern. No one had noticed because all of the passengers had been at the bow of the boat when it set off. The last he had seen of the black dog, Spook was swimming toward shore with the folded flyer in his mouth, Emily's hair ribbon tucked inside.

"The minute Uncle Victor finds me gone, he'll have the whole boat looking for me," Emily said. "Jackson, what am I going to do?"

But Jackson was hard at work on the knot again, and finally—*finally*—it came undone. Emily—her dress all wrinkled and her hair quite messed up—climbed out of the bag, stretching her cramped arms and legs.

"We've got to get out of here first; then we'll think about where to hide," Jackson said, opening the door a crack and peeking into the hallway. "Nobody here just yet. Come on."

They had only gone a short way down the dark corridor, however, when they heard footsteps coming down the stairs. Jackson pulled Emily into a toilet compartment just big enough for one person—*An indoor outhouse*, Emily thought. They squeezed themselves in so tight they could scarcely close the door behind

them. In fact, they couldn't get it closed all the way, so they had to leave it open an inch or two. They were glad it was so dark inside.

Uncle Victor walked by just then, a swagger to his step.

"Must be comin' up in the world," he was saying to himself. "Havin' drinks with the captain! Who would have thought? I get me some of Emily's money, I'll take myself on a long boat trip, finest room they've got. I'll travel up and down the Mississippi River, maybe. Wonder if the old lady's read that ransom note yet."

Emily and Jackson heard him open the door to the little storeroom where he had left the bag, and the next thing they heard was a terrible roar.

"How in creakin', squeakin' creation did that blasted kid get herself out of there?" he bellowed, and let out another roar.

There were more footsteps on the stairs, and then a man's voice called, "Inspector? Is something wrong?"

Emily and Jackson hardly dared to breathe. The captain had stopped right outside the door to the toilet compartment, looking this way and that. Then they heard Victor come out of the little storeroom at the end of the hall.

What would he tell the captain? Emily wondered. He could hardly say that he had brought a pickpocket aboard in a burlap sack and now she was loose among the passengers.

Uncle Victor began to stammer. "Uh . . . sorry, C-Captain," he said. "Got carried away, I guess. But I just caught a glimpse of one of the most thievin', lyin' pickpockets of all time—a girl 'bout eight or nine years old. How she got on board and where she's gone to, I don't know, but I'd advise you to send out an alert to the whole boat. With everyone looking, I'll have her in custody in no time."

Emily's heart was beating fast, and Jackson's was thumping so hard that Emily could feel it against her back as they stood squeezed together in the tiny compartment.

"No, Inspector, I can't do that," the captain said. "I want no mention made at all of a young pickpocket aboard this boat. My customers and actors are of the highest caliber, and my showboat has a reputation as one of the finest. You are the private investigator whose job it is to find this thief and prosecute her, but I don't want to alarm either my passengers or my crew. Is that understood?"

"Uh . . . of course, sir. Sorry. Afraid I was a bit surprised myself. Now I think of it, perhaps I didn't see her at all. It could have been a short lady in a small bonnet."

"Exactly," said the captain. "Now you go about your job and I'll go about mine." And he turned and went back up the stairs.

When the captain was gone, Uncle Victor swore and paced back and forth.

"Emily Wiggins, wherever the ding-dong dickens you're hiding, I'll find you," he muttered. "The only way to escape me now is to jump overboard and drown yourself." And he went back to the storeroom, where Emily heard him opening boxes and throwing things about.

"We've got to find a better hiding place," Jackson whispered. "He'll be checking every door along this hall, even the boiler room. Come on!"

They squeezed out of the toilet compartment and headed for the stairs.

It was getting close to the dinner hour aboard the boat, and it seemed as though most of the guests were on an upper deck, enjoying singing by the cast of the show. Uncle Victor would probably work his way up, the children decided, searching the boiler deck first, then the next deck and the next, where the actors were performing.

Slowly, carefully, they crept up the stairs, their backs against the wall, until their eyes were just level with the floor above. No one was watching. They continued up to the next deck.

All they could really see when they got there were the backs of the passengers as they sat on folding chairs, listening to the singing. They saw the white uniformed legs of the crew standing off to the side.

There seemed to be no place to hide up here among all the guests and crew, so Jackson led Emily back down to the main deck where they made their way to the dining room. Waiters were setting the tables, calling back and forth as they prepared for the evening meal.

Each table was covered with a heavy white cloth that reached all the way to the floor. The glassware gleamed, the silver shone, and a starched white napkin folded like a fan sat on each plate. The waiters started lining up at one end of the large room to fill pitchers of water, and when no one was looking in their direction, Jackson grabbed Emily's arm and they crawled under the nearest table. Safe at last!

Emily was very glad to rest. She was sore all over from bumping around in the burlap bag. She sat with her back against Jackson's, facing in the opposite direction, feet drawn up, arms clasping her legs. She wished she could just stretch out and take a nap, but the music from above had stopped, and the sounds of grown-ups' voices grew louder and louder as guests made their way down to supper.

Suddenly a pair of women's dainty high-buttoned boots slid under the table, sticking out from beneath a green taffeta gown. Emily wriggled her legs closer to her body so as not to touch the woman's feet.

At the same time, another pair of women's shoes, these bright red, appeared under the tablecloth on Jackson's side. He moved just as the woman was crossing her legs, so that the tip of one red shoe was about even with his ear. He squirmed away as best he could.

But then, a pair of white men's shoes appeared on the floor beside the first woman's high-buttoned boots, and a pair of polished brown shoes with yellow spats slid under the table beside the second woman's bright red shoes.

So many legs! So many feet! Jackson and Emily huddled on the floor under the very center of the table, looking back and forth, ready to lean this way or that if a leg moved or a foot twitched. One awful time a large hand reached down under the table to scratch an itchy leg.

How long would this meal go on? Emily wondered. She was hungry herself, and the wonderful scent of steak and roast potatoes drifted down, making her even more miserable. She bet Jackson was starving too.

Finally, finally, the chatter of the grown-ups grew softer and softer as more and more passengers left the dining room, and at long last the dainty high-buttoned boots and the red shoes and the men's white shoes and the brown shoes with yellow spats slid back out from under the table and all the passengers left the dining room.

Emily just wanted to stretch out under the table and sleep. No one would see her there.

But Jackson was nervous. He put his head to the floor so he could watch through the narrow space between the bottom of the tablecloth and the rug. And suddenly he sat back up and whispered, "Emily! We've got to leave. *Now!*"

What in greasy graham crackers had he seen?

TWENTY-THREE

Under the Tarp

"The waiters are removing the tablecloths!" Jackson said. "Soon someone will come over and take this one. Then they'll see us for sure."

Emily was sorry they had to move again. She just wanted to curl up on the soft rug, put her arm beneath her head, and sleep.

But Jackson tugged at her shoulder, one hand holding up a corner of the tablecloth. As soon as he whispered "Now!" they crawled out, crept to the door, and slipped up the stairs to the deck above.

It was growing dark, and a few passengers were still standing at the rail, gazing at the stars. The huge paddle wheel spun in the river. Green and yellow lights illuminated the name of the boat, the *Samuel Cray*, and the calliope played merrily, advertising the big show that would be held at Cottonwood Junction the following day.

Now it was going to be very difficult to find a place to hide, because the passengers were so scattered. Most were in their cabins getting ready for bed; the nearly empty deck would make it all the easier for Uncle Victor to spot two children in the midst of the remaining grown-ups. He could be anywhere in the shadows, just waiting for a glimpse of Emily.

The safest place seemed to be the very top deck, behind the tall smokestacks, so up they went. Emily stood behind one, Jackson behind the other, and whenever a member of the crew came by or passengers wandered up to watch the calliope player, Emily and Jackson moved to the right or to the left just enough to stay hidden. It was very much like playing hide-and-seek in the woods, standing behind the big elm tree.

As the evening wore on, fewer and fewer people remained on deck, especially up top, where the breeze rustled women's bonnets or tossed men's straw hats into the air. Soot from the smokestacks drifted down onto people's clothes, and the ladies said, "Oh, it's much too dirty here! Let's go below!"

Emily and Jackson knew they couldn't stand up all night, moving around and around the smokestacks. Where could they find a big box to hide in? they wondered. They went to the bow and peered at the main deck far below, which fantailed out farther into the water than the rest of the boat. Perhaps they would see an empty box down there.

But no. Standing between the lines and winches was the man with the tiger tattoo, looking straight up at them. For half a second his eyes grew wide and his mouth dropped open, and then he raced for the stairs. The children knew they had only seconds to hide.

They raced down to the next deck. Jackson pulled Emily over to one of the lifeboats fastened to the side of the *Samuel Cray*. He lifted a corner of the tarp cover, boosted Emily up and over the edge, then crawled in after her and yanked the tarp back down just as Uncle Victor's boots sounded on the stairs.

Emily's uncle did not stop there, but ran on up to the top deck, where he had last seen the children. When he came down at last, he was muttering at the sky.

"Curses!" he said. "The brat's still around, and that blasted Jackson kid too. How in tarnation did I lose 'em? I've checked every inch of this dad-burned boat."

Every inch except this lifeboat, Emily thought, huddling beside Jackson. *Thumpa-thumpa-thumpa* went her heart.

Back and forth Uncle Victor paced, muttering to himself. The footsteps seemed to be crossing the deck to the other side, and then Emily heard the sound of a waterproof tarp being lifted. She and Jackson sucked in their breath.

"J-Jackson!" she whispered. "He's ch-checking the lifeboats!"

"Shhh!" Jackson said. "Squeeze down as far as you can."

Emily flattened herself to the bottom of the life-boat so hard that her cheek felt as though it would go through the wood.

A minute or so later, Uncle Victor's footsteps crossed the deck again, and then came the sound of the tarp being lifted above her head.

This is the end, Emily thought.

The tarp came half off, and for a moment, Emily felt sure she had been seen. But at the same time she heard someone call out, "Evening, Inspector. Any problem here?"

"No, no, just checking to see that the lifeboats are in order," Uncle Victor said, pulling the tarp back in place.

"All in order. Checked them myself," the voice said. "You don't have to do our work, Inspector. The captain runs a good ship."

"Of course, of course," said Uncle Victor, and the children remembered that he couldn't say one word about pickpockets, not even to the crew.

When the other man had gone, Uncle Victor did not lift the tarp again. The lifeboats were fastened several feet above deck; it would be hard for him to see the children unless he stood on tiptoe and leaned over. Could it be that Emily and Jackson had found a safe place to spend the night?

They had indeed, and both of them slept well, even though there was no soft place to lay their heads.

It was warm beneath the tarp the next morning, however, with the sun bearing down on them, and when Emily lifted one edge and peeked out, she saw that the actors and actresses had gathered between the lifeboats to rehearse for the evening's performance.

Passengers were not allowed on this deck during rehearsals, it seemed, because there was a rope across the stairway, and the director was asking some singers to do their parts again. Emily felt sure that Uncle Victor wouldn't come to check the lifeboats again right now.

She couldn't remember when she had last had something to eat. "I'm so hungry," she whispered to Jackson as they watched the performers from under the edge of the tarp. "How long has it been since we ate anything?"

"'Bout this time yesterday," Jackson said. "Remember how we ate our beans and corn bread out on the swing?"

"I wish I was back there now," said Emily. "Poor Aunt Hilda. She must be so worried. What do you think she'll do?"

"I reckon she's got the money from the bank—being your guardian and all—and is going to give it to Victor, just to get you back," said Jackson.

Tears came to Emily's eyes as she thought of all the things Aunt Hilda needed for her little place in Redbud. How Emily had hoped they could use some of the money that way!

After a while, lunch was served to the actors. As the children watched, waiters brought up platters of food and set them atop little tables they set up around the deck. There were small chicken salad sandwiches, cheese and crackers, tiny sausages on toothpicks, and pecan cake with sweet tea.

Actresses in fancy hats ate daintily, with napkins spread over laps to cover their satin dresses; men in red vests and yellow shoes put down their trombones and trumpets and helped themselves to several sandwiches at a time.

Peeping out from under the tarp, Emily and Jackson stared at a man's plate only inches away from the lifeboat. The delicious scent of chicken was almost too much to bear. The men and women sitting nearby were laughing about one of the mistakes they had made during rehearsal, and the man sitting closest to the lifeboat got up to get another pitcher of tea for them all.

And what in soapy saucepans do you reckon happened next?

TWENTY-FOUR

Caught!

Emily stared in horror as Jackson reached out from under the tarp, picked up a chicken sandwich from the man's plate, and slowly pulled his arm back into the boat.

"Jackson!" whispered Emily.

None of the actors and actresses had seen, however. They had all turned toward the man who was bringing the pitcher of tea.

The actor refilled their glasses, then sat down to finish his lunch. He stared at his plate for a moment,

scratched his head, then ate a cracker and looked sus-
piciously around at the women on either side of him.
Emily almost laughed out loud, but she was hungrily
eating her half of the sandwich, and it was delicious.

When the actors were deep in conversation again
and two of the men were joking with a third one about
a sour note he had played on his trumpet, Jackson
reached out once more. Emily held her breath as his
hand came back with a fistful of cheese.

When the joking had stopped and the actors turned
their attention to lunch again, the man by the lifeboat
stared down at his plate once more and said, "Now,
what kind of monkey business is *this*? Where's my
cheese?"

The other actors looked his way.

"Why, I expect it's on its way to your stomach," one
of the women said.

"I'd say it already got there, the way his belly's
growing," a man laughed.

"Somebody's been stealing off my plate!" the actor
insisted, looking puzzled.

"They say a gull can swoop down and steal your

food before you can blink an eye," said one of the women. "Better eat faster and talk less, Charlie, and keep an eye on the gulls."

"I'm through with my lunch," another woman in a pink bonnet said. "Why don't we throw some crackers to the birds and watch them dive?"

Emily and Jackson watched helplessly as the small group on their side of the deck scooped up crackers and rolls and went over to the railing, tossing bits of food into the air and seeing which bird would swoop down and catch it before it hit the water.

But Jackson wasted no time. While they were busy tossing food, he reached out and brought the actor's glass of sweet tea under the tarp. He and Emily shared it in small sips—first Emily, then Jackson, one for her, one for him—until it was all gone and they were no longer thirsty.

Later, the calliope began to play again, and there was a rustle of excitement as the deck was cleared. The actors and actresses went to their cabins to rest and dress for their performance. Passengers were being served an early dinner, and cheers went up as the

Samuel Cray rounded the bend at Cottonwood Junction, where a platform had been set up for the evening show.

Jackson and Emily could tell from the noises that came floating out to meet them that a crowd was already gathering, and when they climbed out of the lifeboat at last and peered over the railing as the boat pulled in, they saw that some people had picnic baskets and blankets or chairs, and a peddler was selling lemonade.

"As soon as we dock, Emily, we're getting off," said Jackson. "We'll try to squeeze into the line of people leaving the boat, but you know that your uncle will be standing right there, ready to grab you. You've got to run like the wind."

Thumpa-thumpa-thumpa went Emily's heart. All she wanted to do was get home to Aunt Hilda and tell her not to give away the money. She wanted to see if Spook had made it to shore, and if Aunt Hilda had understood the ribbon and the flyer about the show. She wanted to hug Aunt Hilda tight and never let go.

Emily and Jackson followed the crowd lining up to go down the gangplank. Everyone wanted to find a good place on the grass to sit and watch the show. There was so much excitement about the evening's performance that few passengers noticed the children, and no one asked what they were doing aboard alone.

As the crowd neared the gangplank, Emily saw the captain there at the bottom, helping the ladies in their long dresses to step carefully. Next to him stood the first mate. And there beside the first mate was Uncle Victor, still posing as an inspector.

The captain was shaking hands with the men and tipping his hat to the women. All of a sudden, Uncle Victor caught sight of Emily and Jackson.

"Aha!" he bellowed in his excitement. "There's the girl I was telling you about, Captain. She's a thief, and she's got a lyin', thievin' boy along with her."

"We're not! We're not!" cried Emily, trying to duck under Uncle Victor's huge hands.

"Remove them quickly," the captain growled to Uncle Victor. "I told you I did not want my guests alarmed."

"Please listen to her!" Jackson pleaded.

But no one did, and Emily and Jackson found themselves being dragged across the grass toward the woods.

Suddenly a dog began barking somewhere. The barking became more and more frantic.

"Spook!" Emily cried.

At that moment three men appeared and surrounded Uncle Victor, the same three neighbors who had chased Victor off when he first followed Emily to Redbud. One of the men was carrying an ax. Another was carrying a pitchfork. And the third was holding a shotgun.

"Well, Victor, we meet again," said the man with the ax. "I live just up the road from Hilda, and I'm a lawyer."

"I live *down* the road from Hilda, and I'm the judge in these parts," said the man with the pitchfork.

And the man with the shotgun said, "I live over by the river, and I happen to be the sheriff. You are under arrest for kidnapping a child, for extortion by ransom note, and for threatening murder. We are going to see that you are put in jail for a long time, far away from Redbud."

And there came Aunt Hilda, pushing through the

crowd, her arms open wide, Spook dancing happily alongside her.

"Oh, my dear children," she cried. "I was so upset to find that ransom note. But there came Spook, dripping wet, with the flyer in his mouth. When I opened it and the ribbon fell out, I figured out pretty quick where you must be, and when I followed Spook back to the river, he went to the very spot that the showboat had been docked."

But there were even more people in the welcoming party, because Emily heard two high-pitched squeals, and who should come rushing toward them but the two ladies—Marigold and Petunia—who had once shared the stagecoach with Uncle Victor and Emily.

"Ohhhh, Tiger Man!" cried Marigold, in a purple hat with yellow flowers bobbing merrily around the brim. "Where are those bad men taking you?"

"Ahhhh, Victor, my love," gasped Petunia, with her pink cheeks and her large, orange-painted lips. "Wherever you go, we will visit you every day!"

Uncle Victor turned to the sheriff. "Please," he begged, "make it Alaska! Siberia, even!"

"Sounds good to us," said the judge.

Emily didn't feel sorry for her uncle, not one little bit. Now she and Jackson were where they belonged, and no one could ever take them away.

Aunt Hilda didn't feel sorry for him either. She looked down at the children and just couldn't stop smiling. "I've brought a fried chicken supper for us and a special treat for Spook," she said. "We're going to sit right down, have us a picnic, and enjoy the show."

And blazin' britches, don't you know, that's exactly what they did.

About the Author

Phyllis Reynolds Naylor says that sometimes after you finish writing a book, you feel as though there's more to the story, and so you write another. That's what happened after *Emily's Fortune* was published. Once she got Emily and Jackson to Redbud, she wondered what would happen to them next. Surely the Catchum Child Catchers wouldn't give up so easily. And did you think Uncle Victor was out of the picture? Ha!

Naylor is the author of the Newbery Award winner *Shiloh*. Her other popular books include the series about the Hatford boys and the Malloy girls, which begins with *The Boys Start the War* and *The Girls Get Even*. Her most recent book, *Faith, Hope, and Ivy June*, centers on a girl in Kentucky coal mine country.

Phyllis Reynolds Naylor lives in Gaithersburg, Maryland, with her husband, Rex. They have two grown sons and four grandchildren: Sophia, Tressa, Garrett, and Beckett. Mrs. Naylor is the author of over 135 books. Besides doing things with her family, she enjoys snorkeling more than anything in the world.